A BREATH OF FRENCH AIR

'*I should like to go to France,*' *Ma said.*

'*God Almighty,*' *Pop said.* '*What for?*'

At the end of a wet English summer, the Larkins — now numbering ten, with their new additions of a baby and a son-in-law — bundle into the Rolls and cross the Channel to escape the hostile elements. But it's far from being the balmy, sunny, and 'perfick' spot they anticipated. The tea's weak, the hotel's decrepit, and they seem to have brought the rain along with them. Then the disapproving hotel manager learns that Ma and Pop are unmarried, yet sharing a room under his roof . . .

Books by H. E. Bates
Published in Ulverscroft Collections:

THE DARLING BUDS OF MAY

H. E. BATES

A BREATH OF FRENCH AIR

The Pop Larkin Chronicles

Complete and Unabridged

ULVERSCROFT
Leicester

First published in Great Britain in 1959
by Michael Joseph
London

This Ulverscroft Edition
published 2018
by arrangement with
Paper Lion Literary Agency
Surrey

A catalogue record for this book is available
from the British Library.

ISBN 978–1–4448–3721–6

Published by
F. A. Thorpe (Publishing)
Anstey, Leicestershire

Set by Words & Graphics Ltd.
Anstey, Leicestershire
Printed and bound in Great Britain by
T. J. International Ltd., Padstow, Cornwall

This book is printed on acid-free paper

1

Little Oscar, Ma Larkin's seventh, to whom she hoped in due course to give a real proper ribbon of names, probably calling him after some famous explorer, admiral, or Roman Emperor, or even the whole lot, lay in his lavish silvery pram in the kitchen, looking remarkably like a very soft, very large apple dumpling that has been slightly over-boiled.

Continual small bubbles of spittle oozed softly like pink juice from his lips and Pop, coming in to breakfast after giving morning swill to the pigs, paused affectionately to wipe them off with a feeder worked all over in royal blue daisies and a bright scarlet picture of Miss Muffet, the big spider, and the curds-and-whey. Ma, who looked if anything six inches wider since having the baby than she had done even while carrying it, had worked the feeder herself. She hadn't all that much time to spare with seven on her hands but she was surprisingly clever with her plump olive fingers that were almost hidden in pearl and turquoise rings.

'Soon be as fat as a Christmas gander,' Pop said, at the same time pausing to give his son-in-law, Mr Charlton, his customary open-handed clout of greeting in the middle of the back. Mr Charlton, who sat patiently looking through his spectacles at *The Times* while waiting for his breakfast, took the salutation without flinching.

Nearly a year in the Larkin household had hardened him a lot.

Ma, in bright purple blouse and pink apron and with her dark rich hair still in curling pins, had three pounds of sausages in one frying-pan, several rounds of fried bread and seven or eight rashers of bacon in another and a basket of fresh pink field mushrooms waiting for a saucepan. Just before Pop bent to kiss her full on her handsome mouth and wish her good morning, she dropped half the mushrooms into the saucepan, where they at once started hissing at an intruding lump of butter as big as a tennis ball, cooking fragrantly.

'Mariette not down?' Pop said. 'Kids off to school? Going to be a beautiful day. Perfick. Mushrooms smell good.'

Outside it was raining in drilling summer torrents. Nothing could be seen of the far side of the junk-yard, the woods, and the surrounding meadows in the cloudy, steamy air. Nearer to the house the only visible moving things were a few hens shaking damp brown feathers under a straw hovel, a line of six or seven Chinese geese wandering dopily in and out of a wet jungle of rusty iron and nettles, and a small flock of sparrows bathing with sprinkling wings in muddy pools of water.

This was July, Ma thought, and it was enough to give you the willies. It was a real thick'un, or what she sometimes called bad courting weather. Not that she had any intention of going courting, but it reminded her of times when she had. Wet summer days and evenings frustrated you that bad you felt all bottled up. You couldn't let yourself go at all. The fact that she had let herself go with splendidly fruitful effect over the years didn't occur to her at all. It was just that she hated rain in July.

Pop, irrepressibly optimistic that the day was going to be a beautiful one, inquired again about his eldest daughter, Mariette. She was nearly always up with the lark, out riding or something, and he missed her when she didn't come down. It wasn't like her.

'Not feeling all that good,' Ma said. 'Bit peaky.'

Pop pricked up his ears sharply. Not good? He wondered what it could be? Morning sickness perhaps. He hoped so.

'Oh?' he said. 'Thought she looked a little bit below par yesterday. Anythink I ought to know about?'

Pop gave a sharp, inquiring look at Ma and then a still sharper, even more searching look at Mr Charlton. But neither Ma nor Charley seemed to think it was anything he ought to know about and Ma went on moodily prodding at sizzling mushrooms and Mr Charlton with *The Times*.

'She needs a change,' Ma said. 'Ought to have a holiday. Weather's getting her down.'

'Soon clear up,' Pop said. 'You'll see. Be perfick by midday. Beautiful.'

'Don't you believe it,' Ma said. 'It's one of them Julys. I've seen 'em before. They never get right. By the time you get into August it's like they have in India. What are they called, Charley, them things?'

'Monsoons,' Mr Charlton said.

'That's it.' Ma, with a gesture of unaccustomed impatience, threw four more links of sausage into the frying-pan. 'I don't know as I shan't be screeching for a holiday myself if this lot goes on.'

The sausages hit the frying-pan with the sound of red-hot irons plunging into freezing water and immediately little Oscar began to cry.

Pop rushed at once to pick him up but Ma said breakfast was ready and began to serve the first of the bacon, the sausages, the fried bread, and the mushrooms to Mr Charlton, who was still deep in *The Times*.

'I know what he wants,' Pop said. 'He wants his morning Guinness.'

'Well, he'll have to wait for his Guinness, that's all,' Ma said. 'Like other folks do.'

Oscar cried out plaintively again and Pop asked with some concern if he shouldn't give him a piece of fried bread to be going on with? Ma said 'Not on your nelly' in a voice very near to severity. It wouldn't hurt him to cry for a bit and in any case he'd have to learn to be patient. You had to learn to be patient in this world. Anyway, sometimes.

'He wants his drop o' Guinness,' Pop said. 'I know.'

Mr Charlton, who had heard nothing of this conversation, folded *The Times* into quarter-page size, then suddenly pointed to a picture in it and said that that was a most extraordinary thing.

'What is?' Pop said, 'wanting a drop o' Ma's Guinness?'

4

Pop laughed uproariously, as if in fact it was.

'How many sausages, Pop?' Ma said. 'Four? Shall I do you a couple of eggs before I sit down?'

Pop said five sausages and he would manage with two eggs.

'What's extraordinary?' Ma said.

'This picture,' Mr Charlton said. 'It's a picture of a little place called St Pierre le Port. I used to go and spend every summer holiday there when I was a boy. My aunt and uncle used to take me.'

'Let's have a look,' Ma said.

'This is the actual view I used to see from my bedroom window. The actual view — here — along the quay.'

'Seaside?'

'On the Atlantic. The sea goes out for miles at low tide and you can paddle on lovely warm sand and there's a funny little train comes from somewhere inland and goes trundling from place to place along the coast.' Mr Charlton had forgotten sausages, bacon, fried bread, and mushrooms, and even the cries of Oscar in a delicious ecstasy of recollection. 'Oh! I hope they haven't done away with that train. I loved that little train. That train *is* France for me.'

Pop, open-mouthed, stopped biting sausage and looked completely startled at the word France, as if it were something he had never heard of before.

'France? You went abroad?' he said. 'For your holidays? Didn't your Pop and Ma want you?'

'I lost them both when I was six,' Mr Charlton said. 'I think I told you.'

5

At this moment Oscar started to cry again and Ma said she would switch on the radio to soothe him down. She turned the switch and *The Blue Danube* bellowed out at full blast.

'Uncle Arthur and Aunt Edna adored France,' Mr Charlton said. 'I think they loved it even more than England. They went so often in the end you'd have taken them *for* French. Especially Uncle Arthur.'

In a low voice Pop asked Mr Charlton to pass him the mustard. He could think of nothing else to say.

'It brings it all back,' Mr Charlton said, 'that picture in *The Times*.'

Pop, still submerged in disbelief at the astonishing course of the conversation, now became aware of another remarkable thing. Ma was not eating breakfast.

'Ma, you're not having anythink,' he said. 'What's up?'

Ma got up from the breakfast table. Oscar was crying more loudly than ever, undrowned by *The Blue Danube*.

'Not very peckish,' Ma said. 'I think I'll give Oscar his first. Perhaps I'll feel better after that.'

'Hope so. Terrible. What's up with everybody? Everybody looks pale round the gills.'

Without speaking Ma, who did indeed feel pale round the gills, went over to the pram and picked up little Oscar, who belched sharply and stopped crying immediately. Then she kissed him softly in the nape of his neck and sat down again at the table, at the same time undoing her blouse.

All this time Pop had been silently dipping sausage into mustard, staring at his plate, unable to think of a word to say, but now he looked up in time to see Ma extract from her blouse a large expanse of olive bosom twice as large as a full-ripe melon. Into this mass of tender flesh Oscar buried his face and settled down.

'Was it healthy?' Pop said.

'France you mean?' Mr Charlton said. 'Oh, very. The air's wonderful there in Brittany. All hot and sultry. It was awfully cheap too. And marvellous food. Wonderful food.'

'Did you say hot?' Ma said.

'Some summers we'd never see a drop of rain. And the sea — I always remember how blue the sea was. Vivid. Just the colour you see on travel posters.'

'I should like to feel it hot again,' Ma said. 'Like last year. I haven't felt the sun hot on my chest since that day you and Mariette were married in September.'

'Always hot in Britanny,' Mr Charlton said. 'That's my recollection. You can bet on that.'

Oscar pulled at his mother's breast with steadfast sucks of contentment and an occasional rich, startling plop! like that of cork coming out of a bottle. In silence Pop dipped pieces of sausage into mustard and found himself brooding over a remembrance of the day Mariette and Charley had been married.

A very lovely day that had been, as Ma had said: all light and hot sunshine, with a big marquee in the garden and plenty of iced port, cold salmon, and champagne. He would remember for ever Mariette's striking and unconventional dress of yellow silk, so suited to her dark hair, and her bouquet of stephanotis and cherry-red nerines that appeared to have gold-dust sprinkled all over their petals. Everybody was there that day and Mariette's sisters, Zinnia, Petunia, Victoria, and Primrose, were bridesmaids, each in deep cream, with head-dresses of small golden roses and posies of lily-of-the-valley. Ma, like Miss Pilchester and several of their friends, wept openly at the sight of these touching things and even Pop had a tear in his eye.

It was less than a week after Mariette and Charley were back from honeymoon when Pop began to inquire of Ma if anything was happening yet?

Ma said she should think not — everybody wasn't like him.

'You've only got to start eyeing me across a forty-acre field,' she said, 'and I start wondering whether I'm going to have twins or triplets.'

You'd got to give them a chance, she went on, and Pop could only reply that he thought a fortnight was plenty of chance. He murmured something about the question of Charley's technique, of which in view of his great shyness before marriage Ma had entertained considerable doubts, but Ma replied blandly that she thought that if there was anything Charley didn't know by this time Mariette would soon teach him. Pop said he should hope so.

Ever since that time there hadn't been a day when Pop had been increasingly fired with the hope that Ma would soon have some interesting news to tell him. But nothing ever happened and now at last Pop had begun to have considerable doubts about Charley's desire, or even ability, to make him a grandfather. He thought the whole situation was getting everybody down. Ma seemed mopey and was always complaining of the summer rain. Mariette looked decidedly pale too and even seemed, he thought, a shade thinner and lacked that plum-like bloom that even at seventeen had given her such a dark and luscious maturity.

'Got your watch on you, Charley?' Ma said. 'How long's he had on this side?'

Mr Charlton looked briefly up from reading *The Times* to glance at his wrist-watch. With unconcern he gave another glance at Oscar, nestling into Ma's bosom like a piglet into the side of a vast pink sow, and said he thought it was about ten minutes.

Deftly Ma released Oscar from her bosom. There was another rich, milky plop! as Oscar let go the cork of her nipple and then a sudden complaining wail of hunger as she slipped her breast back into her blouse.

'Let me get the door open for goodness sake, child,' Ma said.

'Never known anybody like him for his Guinness,' Pop said.

'Oh!' Ma said, 'haven't you?'

A moment later Oscar was buried again in rosy flesh, all contentment, while Ma held him close to her with one hand, trying at the same time to pour herself a cup of tea with the other.

Mr Charlton was quick to see her difficulties

9

and got up at once to pour it for her himself. That was one of the things Ma liked about Charley: these little touches of nice manners. They did you so much good.

After Charley had poured the tea she took two or three sips slowly, as if in contentment or deep thought or both, and then made a sudden pronouncement that set Pop choking.

'I should like to go to France,' she said.

'God Almighty,' Pop said. 'What for?'

Hot mustard stabbed at the back of his throat and set him coughing.

'For a holiday of course,' Ma said. 'I think it would do us all good to get some sun.'

Pop could think of nothing to say. He sat in meditative, flabbergasted silence while Mr Charlton let out a positive crow of delight and approval at what Ma had said.

'Heavens, that would be marvellous,' he said. 'That would be great. That little train again, that beach, that warm sea. Those little sweet grapes and the peaches. That food — '

He was suddenly overcome with an emotional desire to strike Pop in the back and actually did so. It was a thing he had never felt urged to do before, but its effect on Pop was only to stun him into a deeper more confused silence than ever.

' 'Come unto these yellow sands and then take hands,'' Charley started quoting, at the same time getting up from the breakfast table. 'I've simply got to tell Mariette.'

Charley was off, Pop thought. That feller Keats again.

'We haven't gone yet,' Ma said.

'I'll call her anyway.'

While Mr Charlton went upstairs to call Mariette, whistling all the way up, and Ma sipped at her tea and little Oscar at his mother, Pop sat thinking. The first stunning surprise of Ma's pronouncement had passed. It now began to occur to him that the situation was not at all unlike that in which Charley, soon after his marriage, had suggested that Pop should give up the *Daily Mirror* as his daily newspaper and start instead to take *The Times*.

At the time that too had seemed a surprising, unthinkable, revolutionary thing to do. Then Pop remembered that quite a number of other people in the village, including Miss Pilchester, the Brigadier, and Sir George Bluff-Gore, all took *The Times* too and if they could do so why not he? Miss Pilchester was as poor as a church mouse; the Brigadier hadn't had a new suit for twenty years and generally wore socks that didn't match; and Sir George Bluff-Gore was so ham-strung with taxes that he couldn't afford to keep the ancestral Gore Court going and had had to sell it to Pop himself for demolition and then go and live in a stable. They were the aristocracy, of course, these people; they were the toffs; but if they could afford *The Times* so could he.

Now he didn't regret taking *The Times* at all. It gave you something, *The Times* did, though he wasn't quite sure what. Ma liked it too, though she still took the *Mirror* herself, otherwise she would never know what was in her stars. Nevertheless she got a big thrill out of the

Saturday *Times* advertisements for rich and exotic foods and was always sending away for lists and catalogues. Such things didn't inspire Pop and he still thought there was nothing so good as roast beef and Yorkshire, rice pudding, lamb and mint sauce, and plenty of roast goose and apple sauce on Sundays. He supposed he might have to change some day, though he didn't see why.

Oscar had taken another five minutes of his mother when Ma pulled the cork of her nipple away from him with another gentle plop and turned him over to lie against her shoulder. The result of this was a series of sudden belches, each richer, louder and milkier than the first.

Ma said that that was better and it must be the gin she'd had last night.

Instinctively Oscar renewed his nuzzling for the breast. Ma said she might just as well turn herself into a four-ale bar and be done with it and gave a sudden deep sigh that had in it a certain note of weariness and even despair.

Pop felt suddenly concerned at this sigh and said:

'Ma, don't you really feel well? Tell me, my old duck.'

In reply Ma could only ask him how he would feel if someone had played football inside him for nine months, but it was a question for which Pop could think of no sensible answer and he was both glad and relieved to hear Mariette and Charley coming downstairs.

'As well as turning yourself into a bar three or four times a day. Somehow I think I'm getting too old for this lark.'

Ma, he thought, had never talked like this before. It struck him as being chronic. Too old? Damn it, she was only thirty-six.

'The trouble is this one's like you,' Ma said. 'Never satisfied.'

A moment later Mariette came in, her dark hair still loose from sleep, wearing a green silk dressing-gown and crimson slippers. In a new state of excitement she ran straight to Pop, who had a mouth full of sausage, mushroom and mustard, and started kissing him with a warm fervour that reminded him of Ma when he had first met her at the age of fifteen.

'Oh! wonderful, wonderful Pop. Oh! you're always so wonderful.'

What had he done now? Pop started to say.

'France!' she said. 'I've always wanted to go to France. When do we start? Do we all go?'

'Who said we were going to France?'

'You did, Charley did.' She turned excitedly to Ma, at the same time kissing Oscar on the back of his neck. 'You want to go to France, don't you, Ma?'

'That's what I just told Pop.'

'There you are — everybody wants to go. Oh! for that sun — ' Mariette rolled her handsome body to and fro under its dressing-gown, her breasts rising in voluptuous expectation — 'I can't wait for that sun. It's amazing what that sun can do for you. Oh! to feel the heat of that sun.'

Pop listened with keen alertness. Perhaps it was, after all, the sun that she and Charley had been missing?

'Ah! the heat of the sun,' Charley said, ' 'Fear no more the heat of the sun — ' '

Off again, Pop thought. Keats again. Mr Charlton started laughing happily and Mariette again rolled her shoulders ecstatically in her dressing-gown, laughing with him. Oscar made succulent noises at his mother's breast and Ma sippped with relish at her tea, so that suddenly, for some reason, Pop felt rather out in the cold about things. He couldn't get worked up at all.

'Is it right they eat frogs?' he said.

'Of course,' Charley said. 'And absolutely delicious they are too.'

'Good God.'

Pop felt mildly sick.

'Just the legs,' Charley said. 'They're exactly like chicken.'

Involuntarily Pop burst out laughing in his customary ringing fashion.

'Hear that, Ma? Frogs! Just like chicken.'

'They eat snails too,' Ma said, 'don't they?'

'Certainly. *Escargots de Bourgogne*. Wonderful too they are.'

Pop sat stunned over the breakfast table, open-mouthed at the sound of a new, strange language coming from Charley's lips.

'That was French,' Mariette said with both excitement and pride. 'Did you know Charley speaks French?'

'French? Where'd he pick that up?'

'Playing with French children,' Charley said. 'Every holiday.'

Ma said she was greatly relieved.

'That was the only thing that was worrying

14

me,' she said. 'How we'd make ourselves understood.'

'He's going to teach me,' Mariette said. 'Anyway why don't we all learn?'

'Why not?' Charley said. 'I could teach you all a few simple phrases.'

Pop was speechless. Charley boy speaking French, Charley boy quoting Keats and Shakespeare and spending holidays abroad — there was no end to the surprises of his son-in-law.

Pensively Pop helped himself to marmalade and made a tentative suggestion that Charley boy should give him an example of one or two of the simple phrases.

'Certainly,' Charley said. '*Bonjour — Comment ça va, Monsieur Larkin?*'

'Eh?' Pop said.

Ma sat in silent admiration at these few but impressively fluent words, bemusedly rocking little Oscar backwards and forwards at her bosom. Marvelling too, Pop said, his mouth full of marmalade:

'And what the pipe does all that mean?'

'Good morning. How goes it? How are you?'

'I'm damned if I know,' Pop said. 'I'm getting a bit tangled up with this froggy lark.'

Ma started laughing, her body shaking like a vast jelly, so that for a moment little Oscar lost his grip on her. With a deft movement she heaved him back into his place at the bosom and said she could never get her tongue round that lot.

'Nor me neither,' Pop said.

'Oh! it's simple, it's easy,' Charley said. 'Just say it.'

15

'Me?' Pop said.

'Yes. Go on. Just repeat it. *Bonjour. Comment ça va?* or *comment allez-vous?* if you like. Same thing.'

'One thing at a time,' Pop said, 'as the girl said to the soldier. *Bonjour* — that it?'

'Splendid. *Bonjour. Comment ça va?*'

'*Bonjour. Comment ça va?*' Pop said, grinning now, his perkiness and confidence coming back. 'Any good?'

'Marvellous. You'd have a jolly fine accent in no time.'

Pop, feeling suddenly proud, started preening himself before Ma, languidly stroking his side linings with the back of one hand.

'Having French lessons now, Ma. Eh? What price that?'

Ma was proud too and looked at Pop in gleaming admiration.

'Oh! Pop, you'd pick it up in no time,' Mariette said.

'Always quick to learn,' Ma said. 'Sharp as a packet o' needles. No flies on Pop.'

Pop, increasingly thirsty for knowledge, preened himself again and said what about some more examples, Charley boy?

'*Au revoir,*' Charley said, '*À bientôt.*'

'What's that mean?'

'Goodbye. See you soon.'

'*Au revoir. À bientôt,*' Pop said swiftly. 'Easy. Like water running off a duck's back.'

Charley said again how marvellous it was and how, very soon, in no time at all, Pop could acquire an accent. Mariette actually applauded, so that suddenly there was no holding Pop, who got up smartly from the breakfast table, bowed to Ma and said:

'*Bonjour, madame. Comment* ça va? *Au revoir! À bientôt!*'

'Jolly fine!' Charley said and Ma started laughing so much that little Oscar lost his grip on the bosom again. Milk flowed down his pink dumpling face as Ma rocked up and down.

'Can you see us, over there, Ma?' Pop said. 'Eating frogs' legs and snails and me talking froggy?'

'Oh! I can't wait!' Mariette said and again her body went through its voluptuous rolling under the dressing-gown. 'I just can't wait. I'll just lie all day in the sun in a bikini.'

'That's what I'd like to take too,' Ma said. 'A bikini. A bit of sun would firm me up.'

The prospect of Ma being firmed up in a bikini fired Pop so madly that he almost shouted at Charley:

'All right, Charley boy, when do we start?'

'Well, the children will be on holiday in August — that's if we're all going.'

'Of course we're all going,' Ma said. 'It'll be education for the lot of us. Like telly is.'

'All right then. I suggest the third week in August. That'll avoid the French national holiday, which is on the fifteenth.'

Charley boy again — knowing everything. Full marks for Charley. 'Perfick!' Pop said. '*À bientôt!*'

Pop, sitting down at table again, poured himself another cup of tea while Mr Charlton marvelled once more how swiftly, fluently, and excellently Pop had acquired himself an accent.

'How do we get there?' Pop said. 'Swim?'

'I suggest we take the Rolls if it's all right with you.'

'Good God,' Pop said. 'Never thought of that.'

'They won't over-charge us, will they?' Ma said, 'if they see the Rolls?'

'I'll get the Beau Rivage to quote everything first,' Charley said. 'Taxes, *taxe de séjour*, service, everything. I think Mr Dupont will be fair — that's if he's still there. But in France it's always as well to fix everything beforehand.'

A great fixer, Charley. A marvellous fellow for figures, discounts, bills, and all that. In the last six months Pop had left him to deal with all paper work, forms, returns, and what Pop called the dodgy stuff. A great help, Charley.

Pop in fact was more than pleased that Charley, after marrying Mariette, had had sense enough to throw up his job at the tax inspector's office to take up more respectable, more sensible employment. It was worse than awful to think of having anybody in the family connected with the tax lark. Wouldn't do at all. Worse than having somebody who'd been doing time.

In recognition of Charley's sensible behaviour Pop had given him and Mariette five hundred laying pullets. That had set them up in the egg lark. It paid pretty well on the whole, the egg lark, if you worked it right. It was another way of getting doh-ray-me out of the government before they had a chance to get it out of you. In less than a year Charley and Mariette had made enough profit to buy themselves another five hundred pullets and were doing very well for themselves, except that Charley would insist on making proper income tax returns about it all, which was a very bad habit to get into, Pop considered, whichever way you looked at it.

As to the house he had promised to build them out of material from Sir George Bluff-Gore's mansion at Gore Court, when he pulled it down, he'd been much too busy on a variety of other larks even to get round to the house's demolition. It would have to wait a bit. Most of his time had been taken up with a big deal about army surplus, the surplus consisting of all sorts of unlikely things like tins of beetroot in vinegar, rat-traps, body belts, brass collar studs, gherkins in mustard, rubber shoe heels, and bottles of caper sauce: the sort of things that nobody else seemed to think that anybody wanted. Pop knew better. There was always somebody who wanted something somewhere. He had to admit the beetroot in vinegar and the gherkins in mustard were turning out a bit sticky though.

But there was no doubt about the change from taxes to eggs suiting Charley all right. Charley had put on a bit of weight and looked brown. He always ate hearty breakfasts and had stopped worrying over his health and whether he was going to wake up every morning with appendicitis or not. He looked in every way a fit, virile young man. All the more puzzling, Pop thought, that he didn't seem to be able to translate it all into the proper channels. He had to admit that Charley had always been a slow starter — but married nearly a year and no children, that was really a bit dodgy. He wouldn't have thought a young healthy couple like them would have found it all that hard.

'Of course,' Charley said now, 'there's the trouble of passports.'

'Trouble?' Mariette said. 'What trouble?'

With as much tact as he could muster, Mr Charlton reminded them all of the delicate and rather difficult situation concerning Pop and Ma.

'Perhaps it would have been better if you'd got married after all,' he said.

'Well, I suppose we still could,' Pop said, but not with apparent enthusiasm. 'But it's a bit of a palaver.'

'I'm willing,' Ma said blandly. 'Always was.'

Mr Charlton pondered briefly on this and finally said he supposed the solution was that all the children could go on Pop's passport, leaving Ma to take hers out in her maiden name, though he was still not quite sure what that was.

Placidly Ma fondled the head of her seventh child against her large cheek, not unduly concerned.

'Well, I suppose if everybody had their rights,' she said, 'I'm still Flo Parker.'

Pop looked painfully startled, almost embarrassed, more at the word rights than anything else, but also as if he were actually being introduced to Ma by name for the first time. It was a bit unnerving, hearing Ma called Flo Parker.

'Oh! well,' Ma said, 'I expect it'll sort itself out in the wash.'

'The froggies are broadminded,' Pop said and laughed uproariously, 'if all I hear is true. Paris and all that lark, eh?'

20

'Leave it to Charley,' Mariette said. 'He'll arrange everything. Not the clothes though. Ma, I'll need masses. I'll need a million new frocks.'

Ma had now finished giving little Oscar his breakfast. The huge melons of her bosom were back in the folds of her purple blouse.

'Talking about clothes, Pop,' she said, 'I think it would be nice if you took your yachting cap. The one you bought once for that fancy-dress ball.'

That was a jolly good idea, Pop said. Perfick. Just the thing for the froggy seaside.

A moment later Ma was putting little Oscar back into the luscious folds of his pram and Pop was at the door, suddenly remembering there was work to do.

'Must go. Got to see Joe Rawlings about the straw deal at half past nine.' He stood erect and perky, holding the door knob, and then permitted himself the luxury of a bow.

'Au revoir! see you bientôt!'

'Au revoir,' Mr Charlton and Mariette said together, laughing. 'À bientôt! Adieu!'

At the same time little Oscar made a series of noises compounded of wind, slobber, and his mother's milk, so that Ma said if they weren't all careful they'd have him at it too.

Outside the rain had slackened, almost ceased. Pop drove the Rolls from a junk yard deep in puddles to a road overhung by oak shadow from which dripped great drops of humid July rain.

Half a mile down the road a figure was walking under an umbrella, wearing a military raincoat of the kind once known as a gorblimey and carrying a grey string bag in his hands. It was Pop's old friend the retired Brigadier.

Like Ma, Pop always felt uncommonly sorry for the Brigadier: always so erect and yet so down at heel, with odd socks, patched elbows, darned shirt collars, and that half-lost, under-nourished leathery look about him. But today, under the umbrella, in the tattered raincoat, and carrying the empty string shopping bag, he looked, if anything, more like a walking skeleton than ever.

Reaching him, Pop drew up the Rolls, leaned out of the window and said:

'*Bonjour*, general. *Comment ça va?*'

The Brigadier stopped sharply and looked immensely startled.

'*Très bien, merci,* Larkin,' he said. '*Et vous aussi j'espère?*'

At this Pop looked even more startled than the Brigadier and could think of nothing to say at all except:

'*Au revoir! À bientôt!*'

'Bless my soul, Larkin, you're in a hurry, aren't you?' the Brigadier said. 'What's all this?'

'Started to learn froggy,' Pop said. 'All going to France. For a holiday. Place in Brittany.'

'Entire brood?' the Brigadier said.

'The whole shoot,' Pop said. 'Baby an' all.'

'Cost you a pretty penny, won't it?'

'Who cares?' Pop thundered. 'Ma wants to go. Mariette wants to go. Charley wants to go. Everybody wants to go. What about you? Why don't you come too? More the merrier, general!'

The Brigadier, who found it hard on his

meagre pension to afford a day in London every six weeks or so and who couldn't remember the last time he had had a holiday at all, much less one in France, merely stood bemusedly in the rain, involuntarily shaking his head and having no word of any kind to say until Pop, with a burst of expansive exuberance, invited him to hop in.

'No. No thanks. I like the walk. Part of my constitutional.'

'Still raining. Glad to drop you.'

The Brigadier bemusedly thanked him again and said he really rather preferred Shanks if Larkin didn't mind.

'Just what you like best, general,' Pop said breezily. 'How about France though? Do you a power o' good, general. Get some sun on that back of yours.' The general he thought, didn't look half well as he stood there in the rain. No doubt about it, the mackintosh and the rain made him look, if anything, more drawn than ever. 'Find room for a little 'un like you in the Rolls. Return trip won't cost you a penny.'

In a low circumspect voice the Brigadier inquired if Pop really meant he was contemplating taking the Rolls?

'Course,' Pop said. 'Going to fly the damn thing over. New idea. Over there in two ticks of a donkey's tail.'

'Good God,' the Brigadier said. His white moustaches seemed to bristle and the stiff prawns of his eyebrows leapt upward sharply. 'Bless my soul.'

'Got to get out and see life, general!' Pop said

suddenly, in a burst of enthusiastic admonishment. 'See how the other half lives. See the world. What about it?'

The Brigadier, who had spent the better part of forty years in places like Delhi, Singapore, Hyderabad, and Hong Kong, had seen all of the world he wanted to see and could only thank Pop a third time in polite, irresolute tones, adding at the same time that he thought the thing was hardly in his line.

'Well, plenty o' time to change your mind, general old boy,' Pop said. 'Get me on the blower if you do. Not going to hop in after all?'

'Thanks all the same, I won't. Only going as far as the shop to get a little mouse-trap.'

Pop said he was sorry to hear that the Brigadier was troubled with mice. Ma hated them.

'Meant the cheese,' the Brigadier explained. He would dearly have loved a cheese of a better, more imaginative kind than mouse-trap, but the budget wouldn't run to it. 'You'll have beautiful cheeses in Brittany. Delectable.'

Pop had never heard of the word delectable. He marvelled silently and then started to push in the car gears.

'Ah! well, can't stop. Must push on. *Au revoir*, general! See you *bientôt!*'

Pop raised his hand in breezy, friendly farewell and the Rolls drove opulently away. The Brigadier, cadaverous, upright, and still both bemused and startled, stood for some time under the umbrella in the lessening rain, forgetting even to say '*Adieu!*' and merely thinking of the delicious,

24

delectable cheeses one could eat in Brittany and listening to the sound of the Rolls hooter, melodious and triumphant as a hunting horn, cutting through the dripping quietness of the meadows, the oak-woods, and the steaming country lanes.

How should he have the mouse-trap? On toast or *au naturel?* Still shaken by the opulence of Pop's entrance, news, and exit, he decided to have it on toast. In that way he could fool himself, perhaps, that it was really *Camembert.*

2

When Pop drew up the Rolls outside the Hôtel Beau Rivage at half past six in the evening of the last day of August a gale was raging in from the Atlantic that made even the sturdy blue fishing boats in the most sheltered corners of the little port look like a battered wreckage of half-drowned match-stalks.

Dancing arches of white spray ran up and down the grey quay walls like raging dinosaurs forty feet high. Rain and spray beat at the windows of the little hotel, crashing pebbles on the shutter-boards. A wind as cold as winter ran ceaselessly round the harbour with unbroken shriekings and occasional whistles like those of Mr Charlton's much-loved, long-distant little train.

'For crying out gently, Charley,' Pop said. 'Where's this? Where the pipe have we come to? Lapland?'

With a sudden feeling of low, cold dismay Mr Charlton stared silently at the Beau Rivage. The hotel seemed altogether so much smaller, so much shabbier, so much more dilapidated and inexclusive than he remembered it being in the last summer before the war. It seemed to have shrunk somehow. He had fondly pictured it as large and gay. Now it looked dismal, dark, and pokey. Its style of creosoted Tudor looked incredibly flimsy and insecure and now and then the blistered brown shutters sprang violently on their hooks and seemed, like the rest of the hotel, ready to collapse, disintegrate, and wash away. On the little outside terrace rows of coloured fairy lights, strung necklace fashion between half a dozen plane trees pollarded to the appearance of yellowish skinning skeletons, were swinging wildly about in the wind, one or two of them occasionally crashing on to the concrete below. There was very little Beau about it, Mr Charlton thought, and not much Rivage.

'Well, I suppose we ought to go in,' he said at last and suddenly led the way with an appearance of remarkably enthusiastic alacrity into the hotel, hastily followed by Ma carrying little Oscar, then Primrose and Montgomery submerged under one raincoat, the twins, Victoria and Mariette under one umbrella, and finally Pop carrying two suitcases and a zip canvas bag.

Pop was wearing thin blue linen trousers, a yellow sleeveless shirt, yellow canvas shoes, and his yachting cap in anticipation of a long spell of French hot weather. In the short passage from the car to the hotel he half-rowed, half-paddled through rising lakes of Atlantic rain and spray. Several times he was convinced he was going under. Once he slipped down and one of the suitcases was blown out of his hands and began to wash away along the quayside. He grabbed it, battled on, and a few moments later found himself shipwrecked inside the vestibule of the hotel, where he was at once assailed by a powerful smell of linseed oil, drain-pipes, French

27

cigarettes, and leaking gas. One single electric bulb burned above the reception desk in the gloom of early evening and this was flickering madly up and down.

When Pop was able to get to his feet again he was more than glad to observe that Charley was already in charge of things at the reception desk. Charley, even if he didn't feel it, looked calm, self-possessed, even authoritative. He was speaking in French. Pop liked it when Charley spoke in French. It seemed to ease and resolve the most anxious of situations.

'*Et les passeports, M'sieur?*'

Behind the reception desk a small, bald, paste-coloured man in pince-nez, with grey, hungry cheeks and brown mole-like eyes, spoke to Mr Charlton in a voice of schoolmasterly irritation, as if hoping to catch him out. But in a split second Mr Charlton had everything weighed up. Swiftly the passports were on the desk: Mr and Mrs Charlton's, Pop's with the six children included on it and Ma's in her maiden name of Flo Parker.

'*Et qu'est-ce que vous avez comme bagage?*'

With a commanding, irritated palm the man in pince-nez struck a large desk bell such a resonant blow that little Oscar, startled, began loudly weeping.

Ma, sitting reposedly in one of several decrepit basket chairs, at once decided that the best way of meeting the situation was to give him a little refreshment.

A few moments later an astonished elderly concierge in gumboots, sou'wester, and plastic

mackintosh arrived from dark regions somewhere behind the reception desk in time to see
little Oscar bury his face in the contented
continent of Ma. The hungry-faced man in
pince-nez looked astonished too.

Pop then remembered that there was a good
deal of baggage in the car, Ma and Mariette
having brought three suitcases each, mostly full
of beach-wear, swim-wear, and summer dresses,
and he followed the concierge into the driving,
howling August rain.

Coming back, both shoes full of water, he saw
Charley in process of being lectured, as it
seemed, by the man in pince-nez. He looked
extremely annoyed and seemed to be accusing
Charley of some act of irresponsibility.

'What's up?' Pop called.

'He says he wasn't aware that one of the
children was so small.'

'Tell him we've only just had him,' Ma said
and moved herself as if to expose her bosom to
larger, fuller, and more public gaze. 'I'm trying
to fatten him up as fast as I can.'

Earnestly, in French, Mr Charlton spent some
moments explaining to the cold eyes behind the
pince-nez the reasons for little Oscar's immatu-
rity. The man in pince-nez seemed not only
unimpressed by this but more irritated than ever
and began to snatch various huge brass-lobed
keys from their hooks.

'And tell him we want a cup o' tea,' Ma said
and moved with squeaks of wicker irritation in
her chair. 'I'm dying for one.'

With mounting impatience the man in

pince-nez crashed the keys back on their hooks.

'He says — '

'Don't he speak English?' Ma said. 'I'll bet he does or else he wouldn't have understood what I said just now. You speak English, don't you?'

'*Oui, madame*. Yes.'

'All right then, why don't you speak it? Instead of standing there talking a foreign language?'

'*Oui, madame.*'

'We all want a nice cup of tea. Quick. And if you can't make it I soon will.'

'But in twenty minutes you may have dinner, madame.'

'I daresay I may, but that's not tea, is it?'

The man in pince-nez snatched at a telephone, as if about to pour rasping orders into it, and then stopped.

'*Combien de* — how many teas, madame?'

'Everybody,' Ma said. 'All ten of us.'

With piercing but sightless frigidity the man in pince-nez stared at the sight of little Oscar busily engaged in taking refreshment.

'Even the baby, madame?'

'Oh! he'll have gin,' Ma said. 'He likes it better.'

With cold and extravagant restraint the man in pince-nez put the telephone back in its place and walked out, at the same time calling to the concierge. '*Dix-sept, dix-neuf, vingt-quatre, vingt-huit,*' as if these were orders for prisoners going to an execution.

Pop stood looking at his new canvas shoes. They were full of water. It was running out of them in a stream. Water was coursing down his backbone, through his trousers, and out of his shirt and socks.

There was a sudden smell of fried fish in the air and Ma, catching it, said:

'Smells like fish-and-chips for dinner, Pop. Why don't we cancel the tea and have it later? Go down well with the fish.'

An old, pre-marital nervousness seized Mr Charlton.

'I doubt very much if we ought to countermand the order now — '

'Oh! no, don't let's,' Mariette said. 'I'm dying for a cup.'

'Me too,' Ma said. 'All right.'

'Like a nice glass of hot port,' Pop said. 'I know that. With cloves and cinnamon. Like I rigged up last Christmas.'

'Or else a Guinness,' Ma said.

A fusillade of pebbles, sharp as shrapnel, hit the half-closed shutters. A cold blast chiselled at the door-cracks and the smell of fried fish grew stronger. The smell reminded Ma that she was hungry. She said so in a loud voice and Mr Charlton thought it a good moment to draw her attention to various framed certificates, diplomas, and illustrated addresses hanging about the walls, so much evidence of the excellent, even high-class *cuisine* of the Beau Rivage.

'*Diplôme d'Honneur* Strasbourg 1907. Lyon 1912 and 1924. Marseille 1910, '27, and '29. Paris, six times. Dijon, 1932. Chevalier de Taste Vin — *Foire Gastronomique* 1929 — '

'See, Ma?' Pop said. 'Cooking prizes.'

'Anything for this year?' Ma said.

Mr Charlton was saved the necessity of finding an answer to this pertinent question by the arrival of the tea.

The tea was in a huge white metal coffee pot, with thick white coffee cups to drink it from, and the bill was on the tray.

While Mariette sugared and milked the cups Pop, moving like a deep-sea diver who has only just surfaced, dripping water from every thread, picked up the bill and gazed at it.

'How much is two thousand three hundred and fifty francs, Charley boy?'

At this moment Victoria started crying.

'You take her, Mariette,' Ma said. 'You know how she is.'

Whispering consolatory noises, Mariette took Victoria out, and Mr Charlton, trying in the circumstances to be both discreet and casual, said:

'Oh! about two pounds. Just over.'

'*For tea?*' Ma yelled.

For one moment her bosom seemed to rise into air like an outraged, affronted puff-ball.

'I thought you said it was cheap?' Pop said.

'Well, of course, you've got to remember — in France — '

'Here,' Ma said. 'Hold Oscar.'

Mr Charlton found himself suddenly holding Oscar. Oscar, like Pop, was wet. Ma hastily covered up her bosom and bore down on tea and teacups, stunned to impotent silence while Mr Charlton said:

'After all, tea in France is probably a pound a pound. Perhaps twenty-five shillings. I was reading in *The Times* only the other day — '

'And hot milk!' Ma said. 'Feel this! They brought hot milk.'

No one had any time to comment on this outrage before Mariette and Victoria came back, Mariette tightly holding her sister's hand.

'Hot milk, Mariette!' Ma said. 'Two pounds and over for a cuppa tea and they bring hot milk. Hullo, what's the matter with you?'

'Nothing.'

Mariette looked white and shaken.

'Look as if you'd seen a ghost or something. Look as if you'd had the bill and not Pop.'

Mariette's lip was trembling. She was taking long, hard breaths.

'Whatever's the matter?' Ma said.

'I'd rather not talk about it. Just something out there.'

'You can't sit down!' Victoria said. 'You have to stand up!'

'Good God,' Ma said. 'Think of me.'

There was nothing for it but to give Mariette the strongest cup of tea she could pour out. This was several shades paler than straw and looked and tasted like discoloured water flavoured ever so faintly with boiled onions.

After that Ma swished the tea-pot powerfully round and round in an effort to bring strength where it was most needed, saying at the same time:

'It'll be mice next. I know. I smelt 'em when we came in.'

As if in answer to an outrageous signal the man in pince-nez appeared out of a door marked

'Bureau' with the habit of a hungry burrowing mole. He busied himself for some moments behind the desk, sniffing and rattling keys, and then asked Mr Charlton if he had yet filled up the forms.

Mr Charlton had not filled up forms. There were ten of them. He now gave Oscar to Montgomery, took out his fountain pen, and sat down in one of the many decrepit, disintegrating wicker chairs. His hands were damp from Oscar.

As he started on the forms Ma called:

'I bet they haven't got television. Ask him, Charley. Ask him if they got telly.'

Mr Charlton looked up and asked the man in pince-nez, in French, if they'd got television.

'*Pas de télévision.*'

'No telly, Ma, I'm afraid.'

Pop was stunned. For crying out gently.

'Terrible. You'd never believe it,' he said. 'Never believe it, Ma, would you?'

'Well, good thing Montgomery brought the radio,' Ma said. 'Turn it on somebody. Let's have a tune. Should have brought the new Hi-Fi.'

Primrose switched on the portable radio at full blast and dance music roared forth, momentarily louder than the wind, now punctuated by occasional thunder, that ripped like a half hurricane across the port.

Involuntarily startled, the man in pince-nez rang the desk bell, setting Oscar crying again.

'Ask him if there's a bar,' Pop said.

Mr Charlton, who in the confusion was having difficulty in remembering the date of his own birthday, looked up to ask the man in pince-nez if there was a bar.

34

'*Oui, m'sieur. Par ici.*'

With one thin finger he indicated that the bar lay somewhere in regions beyond the Bureau, in the direction where Mariette and Victoria had found life so inconvenient for their sex.

'Yes: it seems there's a bar.'

'Good egg,' Pop said. 'That's something.' With relief he abandoned the tepid, onioned tea. 'I think I'll buzz round and have a snifter.'

'Not on your nelly!' Ma said. 'Take hold of Oscar. I expect he wants changing. That's why he's roaring again.'

The concierge came back. Pop took over Oscar. It was now so dark that Mr Charlton could hardly see to write the forms. A tremendous crash of thunder broke immediately above the hotel, setting the shutters rattling, the radio crackling, and the single dim light beside the telephone quaking even more like a candle in a wind.

The man in pince-nez spoke suddenly in French, with a slight sense of outrage, as if still offended by Ma's charge about speaking in a foreign language. Mr Charlton translated:

'He says you can go up to your rooms now if you want to.'

'Well, what the merry Ellen does he think we're sitting here waiting for?' Ma said. 'Christmas?'

Oscar had stopped crying. The concierge picked up the remainder of the baggage and the children their things. Mr Charlton said he'd come up soon, since the forms would take him at least another twenty minutes to finish, not that he'd even finish them then, in view of remembering all the birthdays.

'My belly's rattling,' Petunia said. Zinnia said hers was too and they couldn't stand it much longer.

'We won't bother to unpack,' Ma said. She knew Pop was starved. She was getting pretty well starved herself. 'I'll just change Oscar and wash and then we'll all come down.'

Everybody was ready to go upstairs except Ma and Mr Charlton when a fresh and more stupendous crash of thunder occurred. The light above the telephone went completely out, came on, went out, came on, and repeated the process six more times before going out altogether.

In the comparative silence after the thunder a strange new sound crept into the air. It was that of one of the wicker chairs squeaking, like a horde of mice, in protest.

It was the chair containing Ma.

'Here, hold Oscar, somebody,' Pop said. 'Ma's stuck.'

Mariette took Oscar. Pop went over to Ma, solicitous but unsurprised; it had happened before. Ma had always had difficulty in getting her two-yard bulk into the confines of strange furniture and still more difficulty in getting it out again.

'Give us a hand, Charley,' Pop said, 'before she goes under for the third time.'

Pop and Charley started to pull at Ma, who began to laugh with huge jellified ripples. The man in pince-nez looked on with frigid, withdrawn, offended eyes. Pop and Charley pulled at Ma harder than ever, but with no result

36

except to set her laughing with louder shrieks, more fatly.

Presently Ma went strengthless. It became impossible to budge her. Above the telephone the light came on again, illuminating Ma as a collapsing balloon that would never rise.

'Ma, you're not helping,' Pop said. He pleaded for some small cooperation. 'If you don't help you'll have to go round with the damn thing stuck on your behind for the rest of your natural.'

Ma laughed more than ever. The vast milky hillock of her bosom, deeply cleft, rose and fell in mighty breaths. Her whole body started to sink lower and lower and suddenly Pop realized that even if she survived, the chair never would.

He started to urge Charley to pull again. In a sudden wrench the two of them pulled Ma to her feet and she stood there for some seconds with the chair attached to her great buttocks like a sort of tender.

Suddenly, with shrieks, she sank back again. Another peal of thunder, more violent than any other, rent the air above the hotel. The man in pince-nez pleaded '*La chaise, madame — je vous prie — la chaise!*' and for the ninth or tenth time the light went out.

When it came on again Ma was on her feet. Behind her the chair was flatter than a door-mat and by the telephone the man in pince-nez had his head in his hands.

'*Madame, madame, je vous —* ' he was saying. In distress the necessary language for the occasion did not come to him for some moments. When it did so his English was sadly broken up: 'Madame, please could — Oh! madame, I ask — I please — '

With incredible swiftness Pop came forward to defend Ma. Irately he strode over to the man in pince-nez and struck the desk a severe blow with his fist, speaking peremptorily and with voluble rapidity.

'*Qu'est-ce qu'il y a?*' he shouted, 'and *comment ça va* and *comment allez-vous* and *avez-vous bien dormi* and *qu'est-ce que vous avez à manger* and *à bientôt* san fairy ann and all that lark!'

The little man in pince-nez looked as if he'd been hit with a pole-axe. His mouth fell open sharply, but except for a muted gurgle he had nothing to say. A moment later Pop and Ma started to go upstairs, followed by the children, Ma still laughing, Pop glad in his heart of the excellent tuition given by Charley in various French phrases likely to be of use in emergency.

At the foot of the stairs he paused to turn with pride and perkiness to look back.

'Accent all right, Charley boy?'

'Perfick,' Mr Charlton said. 'Absolutely perfick.'

Pop waved a mildly deprecating hand.

'*Très bon*, you mean, *très bon*,' he said. 'Don't forget we're in France now, Charley-boy. We don't take lessons for nothing, do we? *À bientôt!*'

3

Nearly an hour later, when Ma brought the children downstairs for dinner, closely followed by Charley and Mariette, Pop was already sitting moodily in a corner of the *salle à manger*, a room of varnished, ginger-coloured matchboard and glass built like a greenhouse shrouded with yellowing lace-curtains against the westward side of the hotel. Some squares of glass were coloured blue or ruby. A few, broken altogether, had been patched up with squares of treacle-brown paper and it seemed generally that the whole ramshackle structure, battered by the Atlantic storm, might at any moment fall down, disintegrate, and blow away.

Driven by ravenous hunger and thirst to the bar, Pop had found it furnished with a solitary stool, a yard of dusty counter, a dozing grey cat, and a vase of last year's heather. The stool had two legs instead of three and all about the place was that curious pungent odour that Ma had been so quick to notice earlier in the day: as if a drain has been left open or a gas-tap on.

In the *salle à manger*, in contrast to the silent half-darkness of the bar, a noisy, eager battle was being waged by seven or eight French families against the howl of wind and rain, the tossing lace curtains, and more particularly against what appeared to be dishes of large unpleasant pink spiders, in reality *langoustines*. A mad cracking of claws filled the air and one plump Frenchman sat eating, wearing his cap, a large white one: as if for protection against something, perhaps flying claws or bread or rain.

Three feet from Pop's table a harassed French waitress with a marked limp and loose peroxide hair came to operate, every desperate two minutes or so, a large patent wooden-handled bread-slicer about the size of an old-fashioned sewing machine: a cross somewhere between a guillotine and a chaff-cutter.

This instrument made crude groaning noises, like an old tram trying to start. Slices of bread, savagely chopped from yard-long loaves, flew about in all directions, dropping all over the place until harassed waiters and waitresses bore them hurriedly off to eager, waiting guests. These, Pop noticed, at once crammed them ravenously into their mouths and even gluttonously mopped their plates with them.

Presently the rest of the family arrived: Mariette immaculate and perfumed in a beautiful sleeveless low-cut dress of emerald green that made her shoulders and upper breast glow a warm olive colour, Ma in a mauve woollen dress and a royal blue jumper on top to keep out the cold. Ma had plenty of Chanel No. 5 on, still convinced that the hotel smelled not only of mice but a lot of other things besides.

As the family walked in all the French families suddenly stopped eating. The French, Charley had once told Pop, were the *élite* of Europe. Now they stopped ramming bread into their mouths like famished prisoners and gaped at the bare, astral shoulders of Mariette, Ma's great mauve and blue balloon of a body, and the retinue of children behind it.

Most of the older French women, Pop thought, seemed to be wearing discoloured woollen sacks. The younger ones, who were nearly all tallow-coloured, bruise-eyed, and flat-chested, wore jeans. It was hard to tell any of them from boys and in consequence Pop felt more than usually proud of Mariette, who looked so fleshily, elegantly, and provocatively a girl.

Presently the waitress with the limp brought the menu and then with not a moment to spare hopped off to work the bread machine.

'Well, what's to eat, Charley boy?' Pop said, rubbing his hands. 'Somethink good I hope, old man, I'm starving.'

Mr Charlton consulted the menu with a certain musing, studious air of English calm.

'By the way, Charley,' Pop said, 'what's 'eat' in French? Haven't learned any words today.'

It was Pop's honest resolve to learn, if possible, a few new French words every day.

'*Manger*,' Charley said. 'Same word as the thing in the stable — manger.'

Pop sat mute and astounded. Manger — a simple thing like that. Perfickly wonderful. Unbelievable. Manger. He sat back and prepared to listen to Charley reading out the menu with the awe he deserved.

'Well, to begin with there are *langoustines*. They're a kind of small lobster. Speciality of the Atlantic coast. Then there's *saucisson à la mode d'ici* — that's a sort of sausage they do here. *Spécialité de la maison*, I shouldn't wonder. Hot, I expect. Probably awfully good. Then *pigeons à la Gautier* — I expect that's pigeons in some sort of wine sauce. And afterwards fruit and cheese.'

'Sounds jolly *bon*,' Pop said.

Charley said he thought it ought to satisfy and Ma at once started remonstrating with Montgomery, Primrose, Victoria, and the twins about eating so much bread. She said they'd never want their dinners if they went on stuffing bread down.

'What shall we drink?' Charley said.

'Port,' Pop said. He too was stuffing down large quantities of bread, trying to stave off increasing stabs and rumbles of hunger. Ma agreed about the port. It would warm them all up, she said.

'I doubt if they'll have port.'

'Good God,' Pop said. '*What?* I thought you said the Froggies lived on wine?'

'Well, they do. But it's their own. Port isn't. I suggest we drink *vin rosé*. That'll go well with the fish and the pigeon.'

The harassed waitress with the limp, freed momentarily of bread-cutting, arrived a moment later to tell Charley, in French, that there were, after all, no *langoustines*.

'Sorry, no more *langoustines*,' Mr Charlton said. 'They've got *friture* instead.'

'What's *friture?*'

'Fried sardines.'

Ma choked; she felt she wanted to be suddenly and violently sick.

'Oh! fresh ones of course,' Charley said. 'Probably caught this afternoon.'

'In that lot?' Pop said and waved a disbelieving hand in the general direction of the howling, blackening gale that threatened increasingly to blow away the *salle à manger*.

A second later a vast flash of lightning seemed to sizzle down the entire length of roof glass like a celestial diamond-cutter. A Frenchwoman rose hysterically and rushed from the room. The chaff-cutter guillotine attacked yet another loaf with louder and louder groans and a long black burst of thunder struck the hotel to the depth of its foundations.

Alarmed too, the children ate more bread. Pop ate more bread and was in fact still eating bread when the *friture* arrived.

'They're only tiddlers!' the twins said. 'They're only tiddlers!'

'Sardines never grow any bigger,' Charley said, 'otherwise they wouldn't be sardines.'

'About time they did then,' Ma said, peering dubiously at piled scraps of fish, 'that's all.'

'*Bon appétit!*' Mr Charlton said, and proceeded enthusiastically to attack the *friture*.

Pop, turning to the attack too, found himself facing a large plateful of shrivelled dark brown objects which immediately fell to pieces at the touch of a fork. Scorched fragments of fish flew flakily about in all directions. The few crumbs that he was able to capture, impale on his fork and at last transfer to his mouth tasted, he thought, exactly like the unwanted scraps left over at the bottom of a bag of fish-and-chips.

'Shan't get very fat on these,' Ma said.

In a low depressed voice Pop agreed. Ma's great bulk, which filled half the side of one length of the table, now and then quivered in irritation and presently she was eating the *friture* with her fingers, urging the children to do likewise.

The children, in silent despair, ate more bread. Savagely the guillotine bread-cutter worked overtime, drowning conversation. And presently the limping waitress brought the *vin rosé*, which Charley tasted.

'Delicious,' he said with mounting enthusiasm. 'Quite delicious.'

Ma drank too and suddenly felt a quick sharp stream of ice descend to her bowels, cold as charity.

At last the multitudinous remains of the *friture* were taken away, plates piled high with brown wreckage, and Ma said it looked like the feeding of the five thousand. Pop drank deep of *vin rosé*, raised his glass to everybody, and unable to think of very much to say remarked mournfully:

'Well, cheers, everybody. Well, here we are.'

'We certainly are,' Ma said. 'You never spoke a truer word.'

After a short interval the *saucisson à la mode d'ici* arrived. This consisted of a strange object looking like a large pregnant sausage-roll, rather scorched on top. Slight puffs of steam seemed to be issuing from the exhausts at either end.

Ma remarked that at least it was hot and Pop, appetite now whetted to the full by another sharp draught or two of *vin rosé*, prepared to attack the object on his plate by cutting it directly through the middle.

To his complete dismay the force of the cut, meeting hard resistance from the surface of scorched crust, sent the two pieces hurtling in the air. Both fell with a low thud to the floor.

'Don't touch it! Don't touch it!' Ma said. 'Mice everywhere.'

'I'll order another,' Charley said. '*Ma'moiselle!*'

In silent patience Pop waited, but by the time a waitress could be spared from the bondage of bread-cutting the rest of the family had finished the battle with the *saucisson à la mode d'ici*.

With gloom, drinking more *vin rosé* to fortify himself, Pop waited while Charley explained to the waitress the situation about the unfortunate disappearance of his second course.

The waitress seemed dubious, even unimpressed. She simply stared coldly at Pop's empty plate as if knowing perfectly well he had eaten what had been on there and crushingly uttered the single word '*Supplément*'.

'She says if you have another you'll have to pay extra,' Charley said.

'Better order another bottle of *vin rosy* instead, Charley,' Pop said.

Weakly he started to eat more bread. He had, he thought, never eaten so much bread in his life. He no longer wondered why the guillotine worked overtime.

Suddenly thunder roared again, faintly echoed by the rumblings of his own belly, and presently the little man in pince-nez appeared, making his furtive mole-like way from table to table. When

45

he saw the Larkins, however, he stood some distance off, in partly obsequious retreat, an uneasy grimace on his face, his hands held together.

Once he bowed. Mr Charlton bowed too and Ma grinned faintly in reply.

'Nice to see that,' Mr Charlton said. 'Typical French. He's come to see if everything's all right.'

'Why don't we tell him?' Ma said.

'What do we have next?' the twins said. 'What do we have next?'

'Pigeons,' Pop said. The thought of stewed pigeons made his mouth water. In wine sauce too. 'Pigeons.'

'We want baked beans on toast!' the twins said. 'And cocoa.'

'Quiet!' Pop thundered. 'I'll have order.'

A moment later a waitress, arriving with a fourth plate of bread, proceeded to announce to Mr Charlton a fresh and disturbing piece of news. There were, after all, no pigeons.

Pop felt too weak to utter any kind of exclamation about this second, deeper disappointment.

'There's rabbit,' Charley told him, 'instead.'

Instantly Pop recoiled in pale, fastidious horror.

'Not after myxo!' he said. 'No! Charley, I couldn't. I can't touch 'em after myxo!'

Myxomatosis, the scourge of the rabbit tribe, had affected Pop very deeply. No one else in the family had been so moved by the plague and its results. But to Pop the thought of eating rabbits was now as great a nausea as the thought of eating nightingales.

'It started here in France too,' he said. 'The Froggies were the ones who first started it.'

'Have an omelette,' Charley said cheerfully.

'They don't suit him,' Ma said. 'They always give him heartburn.'

Pop could only murmur in a low, dispassionate voice that he had to have something, somehow, soon. Heartburn or no heartburn. Even an omelette.

'A steak then,' Charley said. 'With chips.'

At this Pop cheered up a little, saying that a steak would suit him.

'*Alors, un filet bifteck pour monsieur,*' Charley said, '*avec pommes frites.*'

'Biff-teck! Biff-teck!' the twins started shouting, punching each other, laughing loudly. 'Biff-teck! Biff-you! Biff-you! Biff-teck!'

Pop was too weak to cry 'Quiet!' this time and from a distance the man in pince-nez stared in disapproval at the scene, so that Ma said:

'Sssh! Mr Dupont's looking.'

'That isn't Mr Dupont,' Charley said. 'He's only the manager. Mr Dupont's dead.'

'Die of over-eating?' Ma said.

Pop laughed faintly.

'The hotel is run by a Miss Dupont — Mademoiselle Dupont,' Charley explained. 'But it seems she's away in Brest for the day.'

'When the cat's away,' Ma said.

'Well,' Charley said, 'I wouldn't be at all surprised if that didn't explain a slight lack of liaison.'

Pop, too low in spirits even to admire Charley's turn of phrase, drank deeply of *vin rosé*.

'Better order some more of the juice, Charley old man,' he said. 'Got to keep going somehow.'

'Biff-teck! Biff-teck! Biff-you! Biff-teck!'

'Quiet!' Pop said sharply and from across the *salle à manger* several French mammas looked quickly round at him with full sudden glances, clearly electrified.

Half an hour later he had masticated his way through a bloody piece of beef roughly the shape of a boot's sole, the same thickness, and about as interesting. He ate the chips that accompanied it down to the last frizzled crumb and even dipped his bread in the half-cold blood.

Ma said she hoped he felt better for it but Pop could hardly do more than nod, drinking again of *vin rosé*.

'Don't even have ketchup,' he said, as if this serious gastronomic omission were the final straw.

Soon the twins, Primrose, Victoria, and Montgomery, tired out from the journey, went up to bed and presently Pop began to throw out broad hints that Mariette and Charley ought to be doing likewise.

'It's only nine o'clock,' Mariette said.

'I used to be in bed at nine o'clock at your age,' Pop said.

'Don't tell me,' Ma said.

'We thought there might be dancing,' Charley said, 'somewhere.'

'There's sure to be a night-spot in the town,' Mariette said. 'Something gay.'

With a queer low laugh and a wave of the hand Pop invited the two young people to look and listen at the signs and echoes of the little port's mad, night-time gaiety: the howl of Atlantic wind and rain on the glass roof of the *salle à manger*, the whirling curtains, the crash of spewed foam on the quayside, and the intermittent lightning and cracks of thunder that threatened every few moments to put the lights out.

'Gorblimey, hark at it,' Pop said and once again urged on Charley and Mariette the fact that they would be much better off, in all respects, in bed.

Mr Charlton evidently didn't think so.

'I'd rather like some coffee,' he said.

'Me too,' Mariette said.

Pop agreed that perhaps it wasn't a bad idea at that. At least it would save him from going to bed on a completely empty stomach.

'I expect we can get it in the lounge,' Mr Charlton said.

In the lounge, in flickering semi-darkness, various French couples were furtively drinking coffee, talking and playing whist, *vingt-et-un*, and things of that sort. A few discouraged moths fluttered about and above the howl of wind and rain no other sound could be heard except a sudden metallic clash as someone lost patience and struck a patent coffee filter a severe blow on top in order to encourage the flow.

While waiting for the coffee, which Mr Charlton ordered, Ma sat staring at the moths and wondering what on earth she and the rest of the family were going to do with themselves for a month. It was Pop who had suggested coming for a month. It would give Mariette and Charley more of a chance, he thought.

Presently, after the lights had taken another alarming dip towards absolute darkness, the coffee arrived in four patent filters, once silvered but now worn very brassy at the edges. The top half of the filter was full of water and the lid was too hot to hold.

'What the hell do we do with these?' Pop said.

'The coffee should come through,' Mr Charlton said. 'If not, you strike it. The filter I mean.'

Five minutes later everyone looked inside the filters and found that the water level hadn't dropped a centimetre. This was often the way, Mr Charlton assured them, and went on to explain that the trouble could often be cured by pressure.

'Like this,' he said and pressed the top of the filter firmly with the palm of his hand. 'That ought to do the trick.'

Pop wondered. Whenever he pressed the filter the top of it scalded the palm of his hand. There was never any sign of coffee coming through either.

'They vary,' Mr Charlton explained. 'Mine's coming through quite happily.'

After another five minutes both Ma and Mariette said theirs was coming through quite nicely too. Pop peered several times at the unchanged water-level in his own with a gloom unbroken except by the arrival of a cognac, thoughtfully ordered by Charley when the filters came. The cognac was, by Pop's standards a mere thimbleful, but it was better than nothing at all.

'No luck?' Mr Charlton said and Pop peered for the ninth or tenth time into the top of the filter, to discover once more that the water-level hadn't varied a bit.

'Better give it a tap,' Mr Charlton suggested.

Unaccountably maddened, Pop proceeded to strike the lid of the filter a sudden almighty blow such as he had seen several of the French couples do. The lid at once went leaping vertically into the air and Pop, in an involuntary effort to save it, knocked the bottom of the filter flying, spilling hot water, closely followed by coffee grounds and the cognac, into the upper parts of his trousers.

'Ma,' he said after this, 'I think we'd better go up. I don't know wevver I can last out much longer.'

It wasn't his lucky day, he said as he and Ma went into the bedroom, but Ma instantly and peremptorily shushed him, urging him to be careful and not to wake little Oscar.

'I'm just going along,' she said. 'Don't put the light on. You can see to get undressed without it.'

'Can't see a damn thing,' Pop said.

'Then you must feel,' Ma said. 'That's all.'

Pop was still feeling when, three or four minutes later, Ma came back. He had got as far as taking off his jacket, collar, and tie but had decided to go no further until he got some further guidance from Ma.

'Where is it?' he said.

51

'Along the corridor and turn left and then down three steps. Mind the steps. The light isn't very good.'

The light certainly wasn't very good and in fact suddenly went out altogether under a fresh clap of thunder, leaving Pop groping helplessly along the unfamiliar walls of the corridor.

When he finally decided to feel his way back he found himself unsure about the bedroom door but fortunately little Oscar turned and murmured in his sleep and Pop, pushing open the door, said:

'Where are you, Ma? Undressed yet?'

Ma said she wasn't undressing that night. It was too risky. She was sleeping in her dressing-gown.

Pop, demoralized, taking off his wet trousers in complete darkness, didn't comment. Life was suddenly a bit too much: no light, no sight of Ma undressing, no telly, no chance of having a cigar and reading *The Times* for half an hour before turning in. This was the end.

'Did you find it?' Ma said.

No, Pop said, he hadn't found it. That was the trouble.

'There must be a doings in the bedroom somewhere,' Ma said. 'You'd better try and find that.'

Pop started to grope about the completely darkened room, knocking against bed, chairs, and chests of drawers, feeling for what Ma had called the doings.

'Sssh!' Ma said. 'You'll wake Oscar. Can't you find it?'

'Don't seem to be nothink nowhere.' Pop was in despair. 'Have to find somewhere soon.'

'You'd better try the window,' Ma said.

Pop, after a few more minutes of groping, managed to find a window. With some difficulty he opened it and then stood there for some time in concentrated silence except for an occasional earnest sigh or two, facing the Atlantic, its wind, and its rain.

During this time he was too busy to speak, so that at last Ma called:

'You all right? You're a long time. What's happening?'

Pop, sad and remote at the window, murmured something about he was having a bit of a battle with the elements. Ma thought this was very funny and started laughing like a jelly, rocking the bed springs, but there was no answering echo from Pop except another earnest sigh or two.

'Are you winning or losing?' Ma called.

'Think it's a draw,' Pop said.

'Fair result I suppose,' Ma said, laughing again.

A moment later Pop brought the long day to a silent close by creeping into bed with Ma, tired and damp but hopeful that little Oscar wouldn't wake too soon for his early morning drop of refreshment.

4

Pop rose from an uncheerful breakfast of one *croissant*, one roll of bread, two cups of coffee, and a small pot of redcurrant jelly in very low spirits. This, it seemed to him, was no breakfast for a man and moreover he had slept very badly.

Outside, the day was slightly less violent. The wind had dropped a little, though not completely, and now rain was merely coming down in a mad, unremitting waterfall, a grey curtain obscuring all but the closer reaches of harbour, sea, and sky.

In the small hotel lounge, behind rattling doors, among a cramped forest of decrepit wicker chairs, Mariette and Charley were looking at French fashion magazines; the twins were playing patience with Victoria, and Montgomery and Primrose noughts and crosses. Several French children were running noisily backwards and forwards or were reading and playing too, constantly pursued by the voices of remonstrating mammas calling them by name:

'Hippolyte! Ernestine! Jean-Pierre! Marc-Antoine! Celestine! Fifi!'

Pop thought these names were plain damn silly and moodily congratulated himself that he and Ma, who was still upstairs giving Oscar his breakfast, had given their children sensible solid names like Zinnia and Petunia, Primrose and Montgomery, Victoria, Mariette, and Oscar.

At last he could bear it no longer. He put on his yachting cap and mackintosh and went out into a grey rain that had in it the chill of December, hopeful of somewhere finding himself an honest, solid breakfast.

The entire length of dark grey *pavé* running along the little harbour was as deserted as the deck of an abandoned ship. Down in the harbour itself the black figures of a few fishermen in oilskins were busy tightening the moorings of their blue sardine boats, on the masts of which the furled sails were rolled like copper umbrellas.

In the morning air was a raw saltiness which sharpened the appetite with a sting. Seagulls made continuous mournful cries as they quarrelled above the boats, hungry too. From a café at the end of the promenade came the smell of coffee, bitter, strong, deliciously mocking.

Inside the café Pop found himself to be the only customer. Presently a waiter who looked as if he had been awake all night and was now preparing to sleep all day came and stood beside his table.

'*M'sieu?*'

'Three boiled eggs,' Pop said. 'Soft.'

'*Comment?*'

Thanks to Mr Charlton Pop knew what this meant.

'Soft?' he said. '*S'il vous plaît.*'

'*M'sieu?*'

'Three boiled eggs. Soft,' Pop said.

'*Ex?*'

'*S'il vous plaît,*' Pop said. 'Soft.' He held up three fingers. 'Three. *Trois.* Soft boiled.'

'*Ex?*'

'Yes, old boy,' Pop said. '*Oui.*'

With his forefinger he described what he thought were a few helpful circles in the air and at this, he felt, the waiter seemed to understand. In a sort of ruminating daze he went away, muttering '*Ex*' several times.

Two minutes later he came back to bring Pop a large treble brandy.

'*Ça va?*' he said and Pop could only nod his head in mute, melancholy acquiescence, deeply regretting that among the French words Mr Charlton had taught him there had so far been none relating to drink and food. It was an omission that would have to be remedied pretty soon.

With increasing depression, as yet unrelieved by the brandy, Pop walked back to the hotel. It would be a pretty good idea, he thought, to buy himself a pocket dictionary and he was about to go over and consult Charley on the subject when the man in pince-nez came hurrying forward from behind the reception desk, mole-like, blinking nervously.

'*Bonjour*, Monsieur Larkin. It is possible to speak with you?'

'*Oui*,' Pop said. 'What's up?'

'Please to step one moment into the Bureau.'

Pop followed the man in pince-nez through the door marked 'Bureau'. The door was carefully shut behind him and the little office at once struck him as being markedly untidy, full of dust, and without a breath of air. Piles of dusty brown paper parcels were everywhere stacked on shelves, tables, and even chairs and in one corner stood a high heavy oak desk with a fretted brass grille running round three sides.

Behind this the man in pince-nez perched himself, less like a mole than a little inquisitorial monkey.

'Monsieur Larkin, it is merely a little matter of the passports.'

'I see,' Pop said and then remembered something. 'By the way, what's your name?'

'Mollet.'

'Molly,' Pop said. 'Always nice to know.'

'Monsieur Larkin,' M. Mollet said, 'I am finding some little difficulty in saying which of your passports is which.' He held up a passport for Pop to see. '*Par exemple*, this one. Mr and Mrs Charlton. This is not relating to you and madame?'

No, Pop explained, it wasn't relating to him and madame, but to his daughter and her husband Charley.

'I see. And this one — Sydney Charles Larkin. This is relating to you?'

That was it, Pop said. That was him all right.

'With the six children?'

'With the six children,' Pop said.

'Then what', M. Mollet said, 'is this one relating to? Florence Daisy Parker?'

'That's Ma.'

'*Pardon? Comment?*'

'That's my missus. My wife,' Pop said. 'Ma.'

M. Mollet peered with startled, troubled, inquisitorial eyes above the top of the grille.

'Your wife? A single lady? With another name?'

'That's it,' Pop said. By this time the brandy had made him feel more cheerful, more his perky self. 'Any objections?'

'You are taking a double room in this hotel to share with a single lady while you yourself have six children?'

Pop actually laughed. 'Right first time,' he said.

M. Mollet, again looking as if he'd been pole-axed, took off his pincenez, hastily wiped them with his handkerchief, and put them on again. When he spoke again it was with an uncertain quiver of the lips, his eyes looking down through the spectacles.

'In this case I regret that I must ask you to leave the hotel.'

'Not on your nelly,' Pop said. His cheerfulness had begun to evaporate. He had a sudden sneaking notion that the Froggies thought he and Ma weren't respectable. He began to wish he'd had another treble brandy. 'Not on your flipping nelly.'

'Nelly? What is that?'

'Rhubarb,' Pop said. 'Don't bother.'

By now his cheerfulness had evaporated completely; suddenly he was feeling hot and bristly.

'If you will leave without complications we will dismiss the matter of the bill. There will be no charge. Not even for the chair that madame — the lady — was destroying yesterday.'

'Destroying!' Pop said. 'Good God, it might have destroyed Ma! It might have injured Ma for life!'

'Please not to shout, Monsieur Larkin. If you will agree to — '

'Agree my aunt Sally,' Pop said. Suddenly, in an inspired flash of anger, he remembered Mademoiselle Dupont. 'Is this Miss Dupont's doing or yours? Where the pipe is she anyway? Is she back?'

'Mademoiselle Dupont is back. I have tried to spare her the unpleasantness — '

'Unpleasantness? Dammit, I thought Froggies were broadminded,' Pop said. 'Paris an' all that lark.'

'This,' M. Mollet said severely, 'is not Paris.'

'Bet your nelly it's not,' Pop said. 'It's brighter in The Bricklayers Arms at home on a foggy Monday.'

'That I do not know about, Monsieur Larkin. I only know — '

'Get Mademoiselle Dupont,' Pop said. 'Go on, get her on the blower, you whelk.' M. Mollet, unaware what a whelk was, stood in a state of restless suspension behind the grille. 'Go on, get her, I want to talk to her.'

'Very well, Monsieur Larkin.'

With no other words M. Mollet extricated himself with dignified stiffness from behind the grille and went out on legs as bent as wires.

It was nearly five minutes before Mademoiselle Dupont came into the Bureau. She seemed, Pop thought, about thirty-eight, rather plump and of medium height, and was wearing a black dress with pure white collar and cuffs: an arrangement that might well have been a considered attempt to make herself look a trifle younger.

'Monsieur Larkin? *Bonjour, m'sieu.*'

She spoke formally, but with nervousness; she played now and then with a large bunch of keys suspended from a chain attached to the belt of her dress.

'*Bonjour.* Good morning. Hope you speak English?' Pop said.

'I speak some English. Yes.'

'Good egg.' Pop felt more cheerful again. He always felt more cheerful in the presence of women anyway. 'Well, I hear you're throwing us out?'

Mademoiselle Dupont, completely embarrassed and transfixed at the sheer directness of this remark, could not speak. She looked unreal. Her skin had that clay-coloured, slightly unhealthy appearance so common in French women, giving them faces like half-cooked dough. Her hair, parted sharply down the middle, was very black and inclined to be greasy. Her eyes seemed, at first, to be black too, but when seen more closely, as Pop discovered later, they were like two thick pieces of glass, carved from an intensely green-black bottle.

'There are times, m'sieu, when one has to exercise a certain discretion.'

Pop, smiling, looked Mademoiselle Dupont straight in the eyes. This was when he first discovered their unusual intensity and the fact that they were really more green than black.

There was a certain intensity about Pop's gaze too, so that Mademoiselle Dupont at once started to play again with her keys.

A moment later Pop put to her a sudden,

simple, alarming question:

'If Ma and me don't mind why should you?'

Mademoiselle Dupont had no answer; she did not even begin to move her lips in reply.

'Ma and me ran away when she was sixteen. Eloped. Spent the night at Brighton. She was thinner then. More like you. More your size.' Once again he transfixed Mademoiselle Dupont, looking straight into her eyes with a gaze of exceptionally friendly, perky intensity. 'Same dark hair as you too. Same sort of skin. Lovely.'

Involuntarily Mademoiselle Dupont drew a deep breath. Without being in the least aware of it she selected a single key from her bunch and started pressing it hard into the palm of one hand.

'Telling you my life story already,' Pop said. 'What a lark. Why should I do that?'

For a moment Mademoiselle Dupont appeared to be thinking in French, for she suddenly said:

'*Je ne sais* — '

'I thought you were going to be a bit sticky about me and Ma. I don't know — bit awkward. Were you?'

Mademoiselle Dupont simply didn't know if she was or not. Pop was talking now in his intimate quick-knitted fashion, smiling all the time, and Mademoiselle Dupont stood listening as if partially mesmerized.

'It was so rough last night we thought of going back home anyway,' Pop said. 'Blimey it was rough. Never thought it could be so rough and cold here in France.'

'Oh! but it will improve!' she said. 'It will get

better! It isn't always so!'

'Will it? Ah! but when?' Pop said. 'Blimey, look at it now.'

Once again Mademoiselle Dupont, utterly confused, appeared to be thinking partly in French.

'*Dans deux ou trois jours* — two or three days. The storms come and go and then suddenly all is over and then — *le soleil, toujours le soleil* — *toujours, toujours, toujours* — '

'*Soleil?*'

'Sun — the sun. In French *soleil* — '

Softly Pop said he wished he could speak French like Mademoiselle Dupont and she in turn stood once again as if mesmerized.

'In July it was so hot you could not bear it,' she said. 'You could not bear the heat on the flesh — '

'No? Bet I could,' Pop said and gave Mademoiselle Dupont a look of rapidity so near a wink, that she retreated sharply into herself and began to think in French again.

'*Et l'orage,*' she started saying, '*vous n'avez pas peur pour les enfants?*'

'*Comment?*' Pop said and remarked that Mademoiselle Dupont had got him there, he was afraid.

Mademoiselle Dupont apologized, began to speak in English again and said she hoped the children had not been frightened by the storm?

'Slept like tops,' Pop said. 'Wish Ma and me had.'

'You did not sleep well?'

'Terrible.'

'I am sorry. It was the storm?'

'The beds,' Pop said. 'And that room. We'll have to change that room, Ma and me, if we're going to stay here.'

For the third or fourth time Pop transfixed her with a smile that was at once perky, soft, and full of disquieting penetration, so that Mademoiselle Dupont found herself torn between the question of the unsatisfactory room and its bed and that brief, tormenting scrap of reminiscence about Pop and Ma eloping and how Ma and she had the same creamy skin and the same dark soft hair.

This flash of romantic reminiscence confused her all over again, so that she pressed the key harder than ever into the palm of her hand and said:

'It is *très, très difficile*. I have no more rooms, Monsieur Larkin. Not one more.'

'Couldn't spend another night in that 'orrible room,' Pop said. He thought of his battle with the elements. He hadn't been dry all night. 'And Ma won't, what's more.'

Mademoiselle Dupont, without knowing why, felt suddenly ashamed. She felt inexplicably sorry that there had ever been any thought of ejecting Monsieur Larkin and his family.

'Nothing for it but the beach, I suppose,' Pop said. 'Bit difficult with Oscar, though.'

Mademoiselle Dupont inquired if Pop meant sleeping on the beach and who was Oscar?

'The baby,' Pop said and added that he thought Oscar was a bit young to start night-work.

Mademoiselle Dupont said, in French, how

much she agreed. For some inexplicable reason she felt like weeping. She pressed the key harder and harder into the palm of her hand and listened confusedly while Pop inquired if there were other hotels.

'*Mais oui, certainement*,' she said, starting to think in French again, '*mais ils sont tous pleins* — all full. I know. All are full.'

'Like the sky,' Pop said and with a slow wearying hand directed Mademoiselle Dupont's glance through the window, beyond which the relentless Atlantic was stretching with still greyer thickness its imprisoning curtain over port, quayside, and *plage*. 'Fancy sleeping out in that lot. Eh?'

Mademoiselle Dupont found herself confronted by an emotional and physical dilemma: she was overcome by a violent desire to sneeze and at the same time wanted to weep again. She compromised by blowing her nose extremely hard on a very small lace handkerchief, almost masculine fashion, with a note like that from a trombone.

This stentorian call startled Pop into saying:

'Sound as if you've caught your death. Well, this rain'll give the car a wash anyway.'

Outside, in the hotel yard, the Rolls stood with expansive professorial dignity among a shabby crowd of down-at-heel pupils, the muddy family Citroëns, the Peugeots, the Simcas, the Renaults of the hotel's French guests.

'That is your car? The large one?'

Pop confessed that the Rolls-Royce was his and with a wave of modest pride drew

Mademoiselle Dupont's attention to the gilt monograms on the doors. These, he assured her, gave the car both class and tone.

'Some duke or other,' he said. 'Some lord. Feller I bought it from wasn't sure.'

At the word lord Mademoiselle Dupont found herself flushing: not from embarrassment or shyness, but from sheer excitement. It was on the tip of her tongue to inquire if Pop was actually an English milord or not but she checked herself in time, content merely to stare down at the monogrammed aristocracy of the Rolls, so distinctive and splendid among the muddy plebeian crowd of family four-seaters parked about it.

Nevertheless she found it impossible to stop herself from supposing that Pop was, perhaps, a milord. She had once before had an English milord, a real aristocrat, to stay in the hotel. All day and even for dinner he had worn mud-coloured corduroy trousers, much patched, a French railway porter's blue blouse, a vivid buttercup yellow neckerchief, and open green sandals. He had a large golden ambrosial moustache and thick, chestnut hair that was obviously not cut very often and curled in his neck like fine wood shavings. Mostly he smoked French workmen's cigarettes and sometimes a short English clay. He also took snuff and invariably blew his nose on a large red handkerchief.

From this Mademoiselle Dupont had come to the conclusion that the English were to some extent eccentric. All the lower classes tried to behave like aristocracy; all the aristocracy tried to behave like workmen. The higher you got in the social scale the worse people dressed. The men, like the milord, dressed in curduroys and baggy jackets and workmen's blouses and had patched elbows and knees and took snuff. The women dressed in thick imperishable sacks called tweeds, flat boat-like shoes, and putty-coloured felt hats; or, if the weather became hot, in drooping canopies of cream shantung that looked like tattered sails on the gaunt masts of ships becalmed.

The English were also very unemotional. They were immensely restrained. They never gave way. The women said 'My deah!' and the men 'Good God' and 'Bad show' and sometimes even 'Damme'. They were bluff, unbelievably reticent, and very stiff. They were not only stiff with strangers but, much worse, they were stiff with each other and this, perhaps, Mademoiselle Dupont thought, explained a lot of things.

It might explain, perhaps, why some of them never got married. It might be that the milords, the true aristocrats, were a law unto themselves. As with the corduroys and clay pipes and snuff, they could set aside the mere conventions of wedlock lightly.

Suddenly she was quite sure in her own mind that Monsieur Larkin was one of these: a milord whose only outward symbol of aristocracy was the Rolls and its flourishing gilded monograms. In no other way could she explain the charm, the ease of manner, the captivating, even impetuous inconsistencies.

'I have been thinking,' she said. 'There is perhaps just one room that possibly you and madame could have.'

'I hope it's got something for emergency,' Pop said, thinking again of his elemental battle the night before.

'Please to come with me.'

With a final sidelong glance at the Rolls — every time she looked at it now it shone like a princess, she thought, among a shabby crowd of kitchen workers — she led Pop out of the Bureau and upstairs.

Once or twice on the way to the second floor — Ma and Pop and the children were all high up on the fourth — she apologized for the lack of an *ascenseur*. She supposed they really ought to have an *ascenseur* one day. On the other hand it was surprising how people got used to being without it and even, in time, learned to run upstairs.

'I haven't caught Ma at it yet,' Pop said.

Following Mademoiselle Dupont upstairs Pop was pleased to make two interesting discoveries: one that her legs, though her black dress was rather long, were very shapely. They were, he thought, not at all a bad-looking pair. From his lower angle on the stairs he discovered also that he could see the hem of her underslip. It was a black lace one.

This, he decided, was a bit of all right. It was perfick. It interested him greatly, his private theory being that all girls who wore black underwear were, in secret, highly passionate.

He set aside these interesting theoretical musings in order to hold open a bedroom door which Mademoiselle Dupont had now unlocked with one of her large bunch of keys.

'Please enter, Monsieur Larkin. Please to come in.'

The room, though not so large as the one he and Ma were occupying two floors above, was prettily furnished and a good deal lighter. It had one large mahogany bed, a huge Breton linen chest, several chairs covered in rose-patterned cretonne, and curtains to match. It also had a basin with running water. It lacked, Pop noticed, that odour of linseed oil, drainpipes, French cigarettes, and leaking gas that penetrated every other part of the hotel. It seemed instead to be bathed in a strong but delicate air of lily-of-the-valley.

'The room is not large,' Mademoiselle Dupont said. She patted the bed with one hand. 'But the bed is full size.'

That, Pop said, was the spirit, and almost winked again.

'And you see the view is also good.'

She stood at the window, still pressing a single key into the palm of her hand. Pop stood close beside her and looked out on a view of *plage*, sea, sand-dunes, and distant pines. As he did so he couldn't help noticing that Mademoiselle Dupont herself also smelled deeply of lily-of-the-valley.

'Very nice,' Pop said. 'I'm sure Ma would like this room.'

'I hope so,' she said. 'It is my room.'

Pop at once protested that this was far too good of her and under several of his rapid disquieting smiles of thanks Mademoiselle

Dupont felt herself flushing again. There was no need to protest, she said, only to accept. The pleasure was entirely hers: and a great pleasure indeed it was. She merely wanted him to be happy, to be comfortable there.

'And you see there is even a little annexe for the baby — in here,' she said, and showed Pop into a sort of box-room, just large enough for little Oscar to sleep in.

Laughing richly, Pop said he was absolutely sure they would be very comfortable in that pleasant room, with that nice bed, with that nice smell of lily-of-the-valley.

'*C'est curieux, c'est extraordinaire*,' she said, starting to think in French again. 'How did you know this?'

Pop drew a deep breath and told her, in a swift flick of description, almost ecstatic, how he had a kind of sixth sense about flowers and their perfumes.

'Acts like a key,' he said. 'Marigolds — I smell marigolds and in a jiff I'm back in Ma's front garden where I first met her. Bluebells — straightaway up in our wood at home. Cinnamon — and it's Christmas. Violets — only got to smell 'em and I'm back in the woods as a kid. The same,' he concluded, 'with your lily-of-the-valley. Never be able to smell it again without thinking of this room.'

Averting her face, watching the distant pines that she had already assured Pop several times were so exquisite in the strong Atlantic sunsets, Mademoiselle Dupont diffidently confessed that they were her favourite flowers, *le muguet*, they were all of spring-time to her, as roses were of summer.

'They suit you,' Pop said and without waiting for comment or answer thanked her again for all her kindness about the room.

It was perfick, he said, he was tremendously grateful, and suddenly, feeling that mere words were not enough, he gave Mademoiselle Dupont an affectionate playful touch, half pinch, half pat, somewhere between the waist and the upper thigh.

Mademoiselle Dupont's reaction to this was to experience a small but exquisite palpitation in the region of her navel. She could find no coherent word either of English or French to say and she confusedly apologized once again about the stairs:

'I am sorry it was so hard for madame — the stairs. But it is old, the hotel. So much needs doing and one does not know what to do.'

Pop, resisting an impulse to pinch Mademoiselle a second time and with more purpose, merely gazed at the rain-sodden landscape and said:

'I know what I'd do.'

'Yes?' Mademoiselle Dupont said. 'What?'

'Pull it down,' Pop said. 'Pull the whole flipping lot down.'

Mademoiselle Dupont, too shocked to speak, turned on him a face in which the mouth had fallen wide open. A moment later she was biting her tongue.

'But it belonged to my father and my grandfather. My family have always owned it.'

70

'They're dead. It's dead,' Pop said airily. 'No use being sentimental. Comes a time — '

'I know we need an *ascenseur*. We need so much. But the money — here in France everything is so expensive. *C'est formidable.*'

'Always raise the money,' Pop said. 'Only want the ideas.'

Mademoiselle Dupont laughed — Pop thought rather ironically.

'That may be for English milords and people who have Rolls-Royces.'

'When you want anythink bad enough,' Pop said blandly, 'you'll always get it.'

This casual statement of philosophy plunged Mademoiselle Dupont into a fresh silence of embarrassment, in which she played again with the key.

'Well, I'll go and tell Ma,' Pop said, 'she'll be tickled to death, I know.'

His final disquieting perky smile caught Mademoiselle Dupont in a state of unreadiness again, so much so that she actually made several quick brushes at her greasy hair with the tips of her fingers, as if to show how calm and indifferent she was. Her ears, Pop saw, were pale and pretty and faintly flushed at the edges.

'I will see that your things are moved. Please tell madame not to bother. And if there is something — '

'Only the wevver,' Pop said. 'The sun. That's all we want. Sol — '

'*Soleil.*'

'*Soleil,*' Pop said. 'Masculine or feminine?'

'Feminine — no, no, masculine of course.

71

Masculine. How stupid of me.'

'Should have been feminine,' Pop said and gave her a last, brief, quick-knitted smile.

Long after he had gone downstairs Mademoiselle Dupont still stood at the window watching the unrelenting rain, trying with difficulty to reshape her thoughts on English milords, the strange, unaccountable, eccentric habits of the English, the Rolls-Royce and its monograms, and the way Monsieur Larkin, who seemed so unlike the English of tradition, possessed the secret of a key through the scents of flowers to events and places long-distant, forgotten, and even lost, as for example with lilies-of-the-valley, *les muguets*, her favourite flowers.

5

After three days the sun began to shine, though not very much, mostly in fitful bursts, still whitish and watered down. A steady temperate wind blew in from the Atlantic, generally raising clouds of sand and at times bristling saltily. The evenings were like December.

From time to time it was just warm enough for Mariette and Ma to shed wraps and sweaters and lie in bikinis on the little smooth-sanded *plage*. Mariette's figure, in spite of what Pop thought about its slight narrowing down since marriage, was well suited to the bikini. Her breasts were round but firm, girlishly fresh but quite mature. Her waist was delicate and narrow, with hips of pear-shaped line. From behind she appeared to have a beautiful little saddle, to which the lower of the bikini's three scarlet triangles was tied with the slenderest of strings.

Ma was not so lucky. She hadn't been able to get a bikini quite large enough to fit her. They didn't go quite as high as Ma in size. But there was, as she remarked, nothing much to them and she had consequently run up two for herself: one in bright petunia purple, her favourite colour, and the other in brilliant salmon rose.

Primrose, Petunia, Zinnia, and Victoria all wore bikinis too, in shades of royal blue, green, pink, yellow, and pure white which they changed from day to day. Ma wasn't having her children outdone by any Froggy kids, some of whom she noticed had their hair dyed, generally red, blonde, or black, sometimes to match their mother's.

On the whole Ma wasn't much impressed by Froggy women, young or old. The young girls who lay or pranced about the *plage* all looked what Pop called pale about the gills; they were very pasty, like Mademoiselle Dupont, and looked decidedly unwell about the eyes; they either wore no lipstick at all or far too much of it in the palest of puce and parma violet shades.

Their necks always looked surprisingly yellow too, Ma thought, a funny suet sort of colour, and she was certain sure they all slept in their makeup. Their hair looked uncombed and tatty and they seemed generally to wear it long, either untied or in horse tails, but occasionally they wore it crimped up, in curious frontal rolls that achieved the effect of making their foreheads recede or disappear.

And their figures were nothing, Ma thought, absolutely nothing. 'Compared with our Mariette's,' Ma reckoned, 'you'd think they were boys with a few pimples here and there. I thought French girls were supposed to be so chick and all that. Blow me, some of 'em don't even shave where they ought to.'

She felt quite sorry for Pop in this respect. There was hardly anything for him to look at on the *plage*. Even Edith Pilchester had more to call her own, Ma thought, than some of these. Even Mademoiselle Dupont had a certain firmness of chest and lower line. She did at least look neat and tidy, whereas most of the Mammas who sat about in beach chairs or even in the shelter of red and white striped tents, intensely gossiping and knitting, either looked hopelessly over-dressed, with two extra cardigans to keep out the temperate westerly wind, or like moulting hawks restlessly awaiting a false move by younger prey.

The young men, on the other hand, were magnificent. Ma had never seen anything like it. All of them seemed to be tall, athletic, bronzed, and lissom. Innumerable protruding knots of muscle stuck brownly out from all over them, accentuating arms, shoulders, chest, and buttocks. Their hair was always perfectly crimped and waved and round their middles they wore nothing but skin-tight pudding bags tied with string.

The young men occupied the beach all day, tirelessly exercising themselves. They leapt in perpendicular fashion in the air, scissoring brown legs. They stood on their heads, did statuesque hand-stands, or pranced about like restless strain-ing race-horses. They played leap-frog or ran about square-chested, like Grecian runners, hair slightly flowing, breasting the wind. They climbed invisible ropes with arms plaited with brown muscle or did long, silent, earnest, dedicatory breathing exercises for the abdomen and chest.

But mostly they played with balls: large, highly-coloured balls, two or three feet in diameter, in segments of scarlet and green, or yellow and violet, so inflated and so light that the Atlantic wind, when it caught them, rolled them swiftly away across acres of bare beach into distances of sea and dune and pine. When this happened they showed new high prowess as athletes, running after the balls in fleeting file or in handsome echelon, Greek-like again, hair flowing, racing the wind.

Mr Charlton, who could see no point in these exercises, was glad merely to relax with Mariette in the sun, reading detective stories or occasionally turning an eye on Mariette, moving her perfect young body over to brown on the other side, like a young plump chicken on a spit. He felt mostly relaxed and contented, even when sometimes aroused by the voice of Ma:

'Fetch everybody ice-cream, Charley, will you? There's a dear. Big ones. Bring two for everybody. And some nuts.'

One of the few things Ma was agreeably surprised about in France was the fact that they had ice-cream and nuts. She had been afraid they wouldn't. At least that made it a bit more civilized.

Pop too was content. He liked merely to lie in the sun and look at the sky. With his hypersensitive, keenly developed sense of smell he could lie for hours breathing the scent of sea and seaweed, sun-dried rocks and pines, tarry boats and fish being unloaded at the quay. He could translate these things into separate living scenes without opening his eyes at all, just as he could smell lily-of-the-valley in imagination and recapture Mademoiselle Dupont clear and close to him.

Over the past day or two it had struck him that Mademoiselle Dupont had become more and more refreshingly attentive. She laughed whenever he met her on the stairs. Was the food right for Monsieur Larkin? Did Madame and the family like it? Were the children happy? Was there some special dish they would like? Pop hadn't the heart to tell her he thought the food was mostly a terrible mistake and that what he really wanted was rice pudding, stewed plums, and roast beef and Yorkshire. He merely joked:

'Ma says it suits her a treat. She's slimming. Taken off pounds.'

'If there is something special you prefer at any time please to tell me. *Sans supplément*, of course. Please just to say.'

On the fifth morning she called him into the Bureau in order to give him back the passports, apologizing at the same time for keeping them so long. She also said:

'I have been thinking that you might care to take an excursion on the 8th — that is, to Le Folgoët. There is a great *pardon* there that day. It is the greatest and most beautiful *pardon* we have in Finistère.'

'*Pardon?*' Pop had no idea what a *pardon* was but he listened respectfully as Mademoiselle Dupont went on to explain its religious significance and beauty.

'Not much on religion,' he confessed. 'Don't care for dog-collars.'

'Perhaps Madame and the children would care to go,' she said. 'You must please tell me if they do. I can give them all directions.'

Up to that moment, rather absent-mindedly, Mademoiselle Dupont had kept the passports in her hands. Suddenly she remembered them and handed them back to Pop, giving a little nervous laugh at the same time.

Pop grinned quickly as he took the passports and asked to know what had amused her.

It was quite a little thing, Mademoiselle Dupont said, just something that had occurred to her.

'What?' Pop said.

'*Ce sont les passeports*,' she said, starting once again nervously thinking in French. 'It is rather *curieux*. A little bit funny.'

'Oh?' Pop said. 'How's that?'

'It was when I was looking at the passports this morning,' Mademoiselle Dupont said. 'It was *très curieux* — very *curieux* — but it occurred to me that if you are not married you are still a single man?'

She laughed quickly and rather self-consciously and Pop, in his customary rousing fashion, laughed too. That, he confessed, had never occurred to him either.

'Single chap, eh?' he said. 'Well, well.'

That afternoon, when he went back to the *plage* after having a short after-lunch nap with Ma on the bed, he found Mr Charlton in a state of unusual restlessness.

Charley, who had hitherto been fairly content, had made a disturbing discovery. He had rumbled what the business of the big sailing coloured balls was all about. They were all part of a design for the ensnarement, if not seduction, of Mariette.

The young Frenchmen, he had at last discovered, had every wind direction beautifully worked out. In that way they could be sure that the balls would always float towards her, so that every five minutes or so they would find it necessary to invade the precious territory of

78

scarlet bikini and naked flesh and, with voluble apologies, laughter, and much athletic show, recapture them.

Mr Charlton made it clear he didn't care for it at all.

★ ★ ★

On the morning of the 8th Pop lay alone on the *plage*, basking for the first time in the true heat of the sun. The sky was actually the colour Mr Charlton had so confidently predicted it would be. It hung overhead like a cornflower, brightest blue to the very distant edges of a sea that seemed to have receded across miles of new-bleached sand to the hazy rim of the world.

The extra-sensory impressions that were so lively in him that morning told him that this was perfick. It couldn't possibly be more perfick anywhere, even to go off to a *pardon*, however beautiful, as Ma and all the rest had done. Only Mariette, it seemed, had shown any reluctance to go to the great *pardon* of Le Folgoët, largely on the ground that it would interfere with her scheme for browning her body all over, but Charley had rumbled that. He had shown swift and admirable marital firmness and had, to Pop's great satisfaction, insisted she should go.

So by ten o'clock the Rolls was away, Mariette driving, the boot packed with a large picnic lunch of Mademoiselle Dupont's preparing, together with several bottles of *vin rosé* and bags of peaches, sweet white grapes and pears. The children now liked *vin rosé* as much as ice-cream

79

and much more than orange juice and Ma was very glad. She thought it was very good for them.

As the Rolls drove away she was already busy giving little Oscar a drop of refreshment and with a free hand waving 'Have a good time' to Pop, who called back that he had *The Times* of the day before yesterday and that it wouldn't be long before he went down to read it over a snifter and watch the Breton women dozing in their stiff white hats and the sardine boats bringing in their catches to the quay.

'Perfick,' he kept saying to himself in the sun. 'Perfick. Absolutely perfick.' He could actually feel the early September heat, bristling with its heavy Atlantic salt, burning his chest and thighs and shoulders. 'Perfick. Good as champagne.'

Twenty minutes later he was asleep on his face and woke only just before midday — a time when the *plage* always emptied itself so suddenly and completely of people that it was as if a plague had struck it — to hear an elegant voice saying:

'Hullo, there. *Comment ça va, mon chéri?* How's the beauty sleep, darling? It's me.'

Pop turned and looked up. Above him a hatless vision, in shirt and slacks of a warm pale shade of apricot, was sitting on the sea-wall above the *plage*. Down over the sand dangled the long, languid legs of Angela Snow, his kindred spirit of the summer party of a year before.

Pop was instantly glad of Charley's brief tuition in French and promptly leapt to his feet and said:

'*Très bien, merci! Et vous aussi,* my old firework?'

'Scream,' she said. 'You speak the language!'

'Just enough,' Pop said. 'Count up to ten and ask for vin rosy.'

'Been dying to see someone who's fun and here you are.'

Angela Snow gave a serpentine twist of her body and leapt down to the sand. Her hair had a glorious gold-white sheen on it and she gave the impression of having chosen the slacks and shirt not to match it but to heighten it and make it shine more brilliantly. Her pretty feet were bare except for flat yellow sandals that simply slipped on, Chinese fashion, without a tie.

When she sat down her long legs curled themselves loosely underneath her. Her clear olive eyes seemed even larger than Pop remembered them and she seemed to embrace him with them as she asked him all about himself, how he came to be there, in this hole, and all that.

'Holiday,' Pop said.

'Not alone?' Her usually languid voice was quick, even eager.

Pop at once explained about the family and how everyone else had gone to the great *pardon* at Le Folgoët.

'Iris too,' she said. 'My sister. Terribly religious, Iris. Got the most Godawful relidge, Iris has.'

Smiling to the uttermost edges of her large pellucid olive eyes she asked Pop, in turn, if he was very relidge.

Pop said he wasn't, very.

'No particular brand, you mean?'

Pop confessed he had no particular brand. He supposed if it came to a definition he would say that being alive was his relidge — that and earth and woods and flowers and nightingales and all that sort of lark and enjoying it and not preventing other people doing so.

'Wouldn't do for Iris,' Angela Snow said. 'Couldn't have that, darling. Couldn't sell her that. She's an Ill-fare Stater. The iller you fare the gooder you are.'

Pop shook his head. Family throw-back? he suggested.

'Got to lacerate yourself, according to Iris. Beds of nails. Fakir stuff.'

'Sack-cloth and ashes?' Pop suggested.

'Dish-cloth and wet-breeches,' Angela Snow said, 'that's Iris. A positive wetter. Even says damp prayers. Sobs away half the time.'

Not much of a chum on holiday, Pop suggested. Why did she come?

'My idea,' Angela Snow said. 'Thought I might find some arresting Breton fisherman to bed her down with. Sort of cure. Don't know of an arresting somebody, *chéri*, do you?'

Pop said he didn't and laughed. He much enjoyed being called darling and *chéri* by Angela Snow.

'And how,' she said, 'are the virgins?'

Throwing back her head Angela Snow laughed with all the rippling limpidity of a carillon about the virgins. She'd never forgotten the virgins. Seven of them and so foolish, riding on the donkeys at Pop's Derby in the summer gymkhana a year before. Almost needed changing still, she confessed, every time she thought of them. Dear virgins.

'Iris is one,' she said. 'The dears do make such hard work of it.'

'This place is full of 'em,' Pop said.

'You don't say?'

Pop referred her to the boyish female skinnies, largely unwashed, who disported themselves listlessly about the *plage*. Ma and he had discussed them thoroughly. Terrible little show-offs, they thought, with nothing to show. And French girls supposed to be so chick an' all. And fast. Even young Montgomery was bored.

'Terribly strict country still,' Angela Snow said. 'Big mother is watching you and all that.'

'Nothing for the Froggy boys to do but make eyes at Mariette.'

'Can't blame 'em,' she said. 'She's inherited all her father's virtues.'

Virtues? Pop laughed and said he didn't think he'd got very many of them.

'No?' Angela Snow said and gave him a smile of luscious simplicity.

Free to look about him again, Pop saw that the *plage* had miraculously emptied itself, as always, at the stroke of noon. In five minutes every *salle à manger* in the place would be full of ravenous masticators. The *potage cultivateur* would be on, stemming the first pangs of the *pensionnaires*. Everywhere the bread-slicers would be working overtime.

Suddenly overcome by a sharp recollection that if you weren't there on time you fell behind in the noon race for nourishment and never really caught up again, Pop half got to his feet and said:

'Suppose I ought to get back to the Beau Rivage. Before the troughs are empty.'

'Any good?' she asked, 'the Beau Rivage?'

Pop was obliged to confess he thought it terrible.

'Bad grub?'

That was the worst part of it, Pop said. He yearned for a good drop of —

'Complain, Sweetie, complain.'

Pop confessed that he hadn't the heart to complain to Mademoiselle Dupont. She probably did her best.

'You must, darling. It's the only way. I'm the great complainer of all time. The great table-banger. And who's this Dupont?'

Pop explained about Mademoiselle Dupont while Angela Snow listened with detachment, unsympathetically.

'All too obviously another one,' she said. 'Like Iris. Plain as a pike-staff, sweetie.'

Pop's insides were light with hunger. Sleep and the bristling air of morning had made him feel empty and fragile as a husk.

'Invite me to lunch one day,' she said, 'and I'll give a demonstration of the arch-complainer.'

What about lunch today? Pop said. He couldn't go on much longer.

'Only place in this hole is Pierre's,' Angela Snow said. 'Out there, towards the forest. About ten minutes, if you don't mind walking.'

Pop said he hoped his legs would carry him. Angela Snow laughed in reply, again in her high, infectious rippling fashion, and actually took Pop's arm in her soft, slender fingers.

'I'll see you don't fall by the wayside, chum. Lean on me, *chèri*.'

Thus fortified, Pop bore up remarkably well until they reached Pierre's, which stood in a clearing where forest and sand joined at the deep central cup of the bay. All his hypersensitive impressions, heightened still further by the growing heat of sun, baking sand, seaweed, and pines, were now fused together in wild galloping pangs of hunger.

Pierre's appeared to be a shack built of bits of bamboo, pine boughs, and old orange boxes. It looked, Pop thought, remarkably like an abandoned coal-shed.

Outside it a few tables without cloths, apparently knocked up out of driftwood, were sheltered by the same number of blue and white umbrellas. Charcoal was smoking away slowly under an iron grid built above bricks. A sign stuck on a pole said *Toilette* and pointed to a flimsy arrangement of almost transparent sacks slung up behind a tree.

Angela Snow and Pop sat down at a table and Angela Snow said this was the greatest place for food you ever came across. The only problem was whether Pierre would like you. If he didn't he wouldn't serve you. He liked to pick his customers.

'Mad on me,' she said.

'Hullo, lousy,' Pierre said. 'Why bloddy hell you turn up?' and then stood over the table to slop into thick glasses two large *camparis* which nobody had ordered.

Angela Snow shook back her sumptuous

golden hair and with her slow drawling voice and luscious smile gave back as good as she got.

'How now, brown sow?' she said. 'This is my friend Mr Larkin. Mr Larkin — Pierre. Mr Larkin keeps pigs — he'll understand you.'

Pop actually half rose to shake hands but relapsed at once when Pierre said:

'Hope you enjoy yourself. What you want to eat? I know. Don't say. Rossbiff, eh?'

This was exactly what Pop did want and his juices at once started flowing madly in anticipation.

'Well, you won't get, see? Today you get *moules, châteaubriant,* and the best *brie* your English bloddy nose ever stank of and like it.'

'Scream,' Angela Snow said. 'Killing.'

She laughed again in her high ringing fashion and Pierre gave a grin part sugary, part lascivious, his thick lips opening to reveal a row of blackened teeth punctuated in the centre by a positive door-knob of gold. The rest of his sunburnt body, which Pop thought was almost as wide as Ma's, suffered from these same unclean extravagances. His blue-striped sweat shirt seemed to have been dipped in candle-grease. His uncut black hair could have been knotted in his neck. Glimpses of a belly both hairy and sweaty appeared from time to time between the bottom edge of his shirt and the tops of his trousers, which were held up by some sort of bell-rope, bright scarlet and hung with gilded tassels.

'And what wine you want?'

'Vin rosy,' Pop said.

'Rosy, rosy, rosy,' Pierre said. 'Well, we don't

have rosy, rosy, rosy. Here you bloddy well have what you get and like it.'

'Mad,' Angela Snow said. 'Killing me.'

Pop thought it would kill him too and was openly relieved when Pierre went away, dragging one foot, like a pot-bellied crab crawling across the sand.

'Going to bring Iris here one day,' Angela Snow said. 'Pierre's the type for her. Half an hour with him and she'd never be the same again.'

Pop was positive she wouldn't be.

'Fun, isn't it?' Angela Snow said. 'Don't you think so? Awful fun. And the food celestial.'

Pop was busy drinking *campari* for the first time and decided he didn't like it.

'These are the only places,' Angela Snow said. 'Real France. All the atmosphere. Piquant somehow — delish.'

Scooping up his mussels and thinking, like Ma, that he wasn't going to get very fat on this lark, Pop watched Pierre grilling the *châteaubriant* over a glowing bed of charcoal. Now and then Pierre scratched his long black hair or the hairs on his chest and sometimes he spat over the grill into the sand.

Watching him, Pop was reminded of Charley's opinion that the French were the *élite* of Europe. France was the place. Everything so cultured.

'Two bloddy steaks for two bloddy English. *Bon appétit.*'

A certain belching contempt filled the glowing autumn air. This, however, was merely yet another signal for Angela Snow to break into fresh peals of laughter and say what awful fun it was.

'A change from the deadly Dupont and all that anyway, darling,' she said.

It certainly was, Pop said, and then turned with intense relish to tackle the *châteaubriant* and its accompanying *pommes frites*. After a struggle of five minutes or so it struck him that the meat was, perhaps, a piece of dog. The charred rectangle, when cut, was icy blue inside and exuded large quantities of blood. This, like the *pommes frites*, was stone cold. The inner sinews of the meat itself, so tenaciously bound to each other that nothing could separate them, were stone cold too.

'Terribly naughty of me,' Angela Snow said. 'You'd have liked mustard, wouldn't you?'

Pop still struggling, said it didn't matter. Nevertheless Angela Snow said she'd ask for it, and it turned out to be English when it came.

'Suppose it's *très snob*, wouldn't you think perhaps?' she said. 'English mustard?'

Pop, masticating hard at bits of dog, supposed it was. *Très snob* — rather good expression, he thought. He must tell Ma.

'How about some cheese? Or fruit perhaps?'

Pop, who was feeling a little less light, but not much, said he fancied both.

For the next half hour it was delicious to sit in the open air, on the edge of the pines, and eat cheese, peel big yellow peaches, and suck grapes; and also, Pop thought, to watch newly arrived customers struggling with their rectangles of charred dog.

Now and then Pierre, ruder and louder as he warmed up to his work, poured brandy over the *châteaubriants* and set them alight. Dramatic flames shot into the air, making the customers look keener than ever in anticipation. Pop enjoyed watching this and made Angela Snow laugh ringingly by saying that he supposed this was the way you made hot dog.

'And coffee. What will you have with your coffee?'

Pop said he fancied a Rolls-Royce.

'One of your blinders?'

Pop said it was; though Red Bull was stronger.

'You think Pierre can mix it?'

'Easy,' Pop said. 'Half vermouth, quarter whisky, quarter gin, dash of orange bitters.'

'That'll suit me too,' she said.

'Better make 'em doubles,' Pop said. 'Easier somehow.'

Pierre seemed unexpectedly impressed by the privilege of mixing strange and special drinks and momentarily dropped all rudeness to become softly, almost obsequiously polite: probably, Pop thought, because it was another case of *très snob*.

Out in the bay the copper sails of departing fishing boats lit up the blue cornflower of sky with such intensity in the sunlight that they too were triangles of fire. All illumination too, Angela Snow's hair seemed to shine more beautifully when broken pine shadow crossed it and left it free again as the sun moved over the sand.

Soon the double Rolls-Royces had made Pop feel more like himself and he responded with an involuntary belch and a robust 'Perfick!' when Angela Snow suggested a short siesta in the dunes.

'I'll get the bill,' he said.

'No, no,' she said. 'My party.'

'Not on your nelly,' Pop said.

'Darling, that's not nice. I asked you.'

'I'm paying,' Pop said with all his charm. 'You think I don't know my technique? Rhubarb.'

When the bill came Pop looked at it and suddenly felt cold. There were so many items and figures that he could neither disentangle them nor add them up. His eye merely grasped at a few painful essentials and blinked the rest.

The portions of charred dog had each cost 1,200 francs; the *moules marinières* 700 francs; the cheese 500 francs; the double Rolls-Royces each 1,400 francs, making a final total, with tax on top of service and supplement on top of tax, of 11,650 francs.

As he fumbled to pay this, a last alarming item caught his eye.

'What's *couvert*?' he said. 'What the blazes is *couvert*? We never had *couvert*.'

Angela Snow laughed in her most celestial fashion.

'That,' she explained to him, 'was just the breathing charge.'

Pop, who was never one to be unduly miserable over the cost of pleasure, thought this was very funny and was still laughing loudly about it when they reached the dunes. He must tell Ma that one: the *très snob* lark and the breathing charge. Jolly good, both of them.

He was still more delighted when Angela Snow's first act on reaching the sand dunes was to cast off her shirt and drop her apricot slacks and stand before him in a yellow bikini so sparsely cut that nothing really separated her from pure golden nakedness.

'My God, this is good,' she said and lay flat on her back in a nest of sand. 'This is good. Where are you?'

Pop didn't know quite where he was. He felt more than slightly lost and dazzled.

'Come and lie down with me, *chéri*. Come on.'

This invitation was delivered with such bewitching languor that Pop was at her side, half in a dream, before he really knew it. Almost at once she closed her eyes. The deep olive lids, shutting out the large pellucid eyes that were always so warm and embracing, seemed now to offer him the further invitation to take in the whole pattern of her long slender body: the slim beautiful legs and arms, the sloping shoulders and the tiny perfectly scooped salt-cellars below the neck, the small but upright breasts, and the navel reposing centrally below them like, Pop thought, a perfick little winkle shell.

As if knowing quite well that he was taking his fill of these things, and with some pleasure, she let her eyes remain closed for fully two minutes before opening them again.

Then she smiled: still a languid smile but also rather fixed.

'Suppose you know I'm madly in love with you?'

Pop confessed he didn't know. It was news.

'Outrageously. All-consuming,' she said. 'Night and day.'

'Jolly good,' Pop said. 'Perfick.'

'Not on your nelly,' she said. 'It's hell.'

A recurrent lick or two of fire from the Rolls-Royce raced about Pop's veins and caused him to say that this was crazy.

'Right first time,' she said. 'Crazy. Mad. Mad as those hares.'

For crying out gently, Pop thought. That was bad. By the way, had she ever seen those hares?

'No,' she said. 'Tell me.'

Watching those pellucid olive eyes that now seemed to have added a look of mystery to their largeness, Pop told her about the hares: the strange wild gambollings that you would see in March, the leaping, dancing business of spring courtship.

'Fascinating,' she said. 'That would be a thrill.'

'Bit mysterious,' Pop said. 'All that tearing about and dancing.'

'Not more than us,' she said. 'What do we dance for? I mean all that stuff in Freud.'

What, she asked, did he feel about Freud?

'Never touch it,' Pop said.

'Scream,' she said. 'I love you.'

She laughed so much at this that it was fully a minute before she was calm again and said:

'Here's me madly in love with you ever since that virgin-firework lark and you've never even kissed me.'

This was a state of affairs, Pop said, that could be remedied with no delay at all.

A second later he was lying at her side, kissing her for the first time. He had always been a great believer in first times, his theory being that there might never be another, especially where women were concerned, and now, with velvet artistry, one hand softly under her small left breast, he made the kiss last for ten minutes or more.

This experience left even Angela Snow slightly light-headed. She seemed to come round, already slightly tipsy after the wine, as if after a deep, passionate faint. Her large eyes blinked slowly, in a dream, and there might even have been a tear of emotion in them as she smiled.

He must save one of those for Iris sometime, she said in a languid attempt at light-heartedness, and what a lucky creature his wife was.

It was essential to keep all those things, Pop thought, on a light-hearted level. Else it wouldn't be fair to Ma. This now seemed the critical moment with Angela Snow and he laughed resoundingly.

'What's funny?' she said.

'Well,' Pop said, 'if everybody had their right I haven't got a wife.'

'Joke.'

It certainly was a bit of a lark, Pop said, when you thought of it. Him and Ma not married. And Ma on a separate passport an' all. Did Angela mean she'd never heard?

'Not a peep,' she said. She'd concluded from the offspring alone that all was well.

'Must get it done some day,' Pop said. 'No good. You know we've had another since I saw you?'

Unsurprised, Angela Snow held him in a gaze

93

fully recovered from its first emotional storm and said with languor:

'Good show. Means you're still agile, virile, and fertile.'

Pop said he hoped so and was so amused and even slightly flattered that he granted her the indulgence of a second kiss, holding her right breast this time, again with prolonged tenderness.

Passion and fervour left their mark on Angela Snow even more deeply than before and as she came round a second time she again felt it necessary to check emotion with yet another touch of flippancy.

'Don't know which I liked best. The one from the married man I had first, or the single one I had second.'

'Mademoiselle Dupont knows I'm not married too. Rumbled it from the passports.'

'Oh! she does, does she?'

And once again she gave him a smile of luscious, penetrative simplicity.

They lay on the dunes, watching the sun across the bay and occasional triangles of sail-fire cut across the blue horizon, for the rest of the afternoon. As time went on her almost naked body grew warmer and warmer in the sun. The sand of the dunes became quite hot to the touch as the sun swung westwards and most of the time Pop couldn't help thinking what a beautiful place it would be for Mariette and Charley to try out sometime. It might encourage them a bit.

At last, when it was time to go, Angela Snow said:

'See you soon, poppet. Don't let it be long. The nerves won't stand it.'

'Come and have lunch at the hotel one day,' Pop said. 'Ma'd love to see you.'

'Even the hotel,' she said. 'Anywhere. But don't let it be long.'

Finally, with a long quiet sigh, she drew on her slacks and Pop said goodbye to what he thought, with pleasure but detachment, was the nicest body he had ever seen since he first met Ma.

That night, as he sat in bed reading *The Times* and smoking his late cigar, he broke off several times from reading to tell Ma about Angela Snow, the terrible lunch, the bill, the *très snob* lark, and the breathing charge.

Ma said she was very pleased about Angela Snow; it had made his afternoon.

'Get round to kissing her?'

Pop confessed that he had but Ma, huge and restful in transparent nightgown after a day that had been a strange mixture of religion and fair, French fish-and-chips and saints, remained quietly unperturbed.

'Says she's in love with me.'

'That pleased you, I'll bet. Nice girl. I like her. Bit of a card.'

For the third or fourth time that evening Pop remarked that he was thirsty. He expected it was the mussels. All shell-fish made him thirsty.

'Well, go down and get a drink,' Ma said. 'Bring me one too.'

Pop said this was a good idea and got out of bed to put on a silk dressing-gown vividly embroidered in green and purple with vast Asiatic dragons, a last minute holiday present from Ma, remembering something else as he did so:

'Ma, you remember that lot of pickled cucumbers, gherkins or whatever they were I had left over from that army surplus deal? The one I made nearly six thousand out of?'

'The ones you got stored in the top barn?' Ma said. 'I know.'

Pop chuckled ripely.

'Hocked 'em all to one of the fishing boat skippers this afternoon after Angela had gone,' he said. 'Seems they're just what they want to pep up their diet with. Terrible monotonous diet they have, these Froggy fishermen. Potatoes and fish all boiled up together. Saw 'em doing it. And gallons of wine.'

'Hope you'll get paid.'

'Coming over to pick 'em up himself and pay me,' Pop said. 'Puts in to Shoreham sometimes. What do you want — champagne?'

'Just what I could do with,' Ma said.

Pop, going downstairs, found Mademoiselle Dupont going over her books in the Bureau. She got up to greet him in her customary nervous fashion, fearing another complaint, but Pop at once put her at rest by explaining about the champagne.

'And what mark of champagne do you prefer, Monsieur Larkin?'

The best champagne Pop could ever recall drinking was something called Bollinger '29 at a big Hunt Ball at home, just before the war.

He mentioned this but Mademoiselle Dupont shook her head. 'In all France I do not think you could now find one bottle of Bollinger '29. All is past of that year.'

'Pity,' Pop said.

'But I have Bollinger '34. That too is good.'

That, Pop said, would do him all right.

Later he insisted on carrying it upstairs himself: ice-bucket and bottle and glasses on a tray. As he did so Mademoiselle Dupont stood in her habitual position at the foot of the stairs and watched him in soft admiration, dreamily thinking.

Day by day it was becoming increasingly clear to her that Monsieur Larkin was a milord. Only a milord could smoke such expensive cigars in bed at night and ask for Bollinger '29. Only a milord could walk the quayside with such an elegant lady as she had seen him pass the hotel with that afternoon: so golden and aristocratic in her elegant apricot slacks.

At the turn of the stairs Pop turned, cocked his head to one side, and looked back.

'*Bonsoir, Mademoiselle, dormez bien,*' he said nippily. 'Sleep well.'

'*Bonsoir,*' she said. 'Sleep well, milord.'

Pop thought that this milord lark just about took the biscuit and he told Ma all about it as he uncorked the champagne in the bedroom.

'Called me my lord, Ma,' he said. 'What price that?'

Ma, who sat up in bed popping Chanel No. 5 down her bosom, thought it was a scream.

'Lord Larkin,' she said. 'Sounds all right, though. Not half bad. I think it sounds perfick, don't you?'

Pop said he certainly did and, laughing softly, poured out the champagne. In fact it was more than perfick.

'I think it's jolly *très snob*, Ma,' he said, 'don't you? Very *très snob*.'

6

Pop began to watch events on the *plage* with growing uneasiness, if not dismay. Things were not going well at all. It was clear as daylight that Mariette and Charley were right off hooks.

Periodically he talked to Ma about it, but Ma seemed quite indifferent, beautifully unperturbed. With great placidity she sat all day watching the sea, the French mammas, the leaping young gods, the tatty little French girls, and the fishing boats putting out to sea. She knitted, read magazines, sun-bathed, and gave little Oscar the refreshment he needed, serenely unconcerned.

'What's Mariette sulking for?' Pop wanted to know. 'Dammit, she hardly speaks to Charley nowadays.'

Ma made the astonishing suggestion that it was probably lack of variety.

'Variety?' Pop said. This was beyond him. 'Variety in what?'

'Before she was married she never had less than two or three running after her,' Ma said. 'Now she's only got Charley.'

Pop, who had never looked at it in this way, had nothing to say and Ma went on:

'What do you think I let you run around with Angela Snow and old Edith Pilchester for?'

Pop said blandly he hadn't the foggiest.

'Variety,' Ma said serenely. 'Variety.'

Pop still couldn't understand why Mariette should always seem to be sulking. At this rate he and Ma would be fifty before they had any grandchildren: a terrible thing. Why were them two always off hooks? Did Ma think that it was possibly some defect in Charley's technique? And if so should he have a quiet word with Charley on the matter?

'Don't you do no such thing,' Ma said. 'I've had a word already.'

'With Charley?'

'No: with Mariette.'

Setting aside the notion that perhaps the whole matter was bound up in some curious feminine secret, Pop said:

'Give her any ideas?'

'Yes,' Ma said. 'I did. I told her to start flirting.'

Pop whistled. Even he was stunned with surprise.

Ma said she didn't see that there was anything to be surprised about. Even the twins and Primrose flirted. Even Victoria had started. Didn't Pop use his optics nowadays? Hadn't he seen Zinnia and Petunia making eyes at those two little black-eyed French boys who wore such funny little pinafores? They were at it all day. They had them in a tizzy.

'Flirting's good for people,' Ma said. 'It's like a tonic. You ought to know.'

Pop laughed and asked Ma if she'd thought of going in for a little herself.

'I might,' she said. 'Only it's a bit difficult with Oscar.'

Pop was pleased at this and asked Ma if she

thought a little drop of flirting now and then would do Charley any harm?

'Flirting with who?' Ma, who was sitting placidly on the sand, huge pale legs outstretched, indicated with a contemptuous wave of her heavily ringed fingers the pallid creatures who populated the *plage* on every side. 'With this tatty lot? I pity him.'

Pop said he was thinking more of somebody like Angela Snow. She could teach him a thing or two.

'You should know,' she said. 'He's not her type, though. Not like you are.'

'She's got a sister,' Pop said. 'Very religious.'

'Give the poor chap a chance,' she said. 'I'm trying to make it easy for him. Not — '

She broke off and looked at her wrist-watch. It was ten o'clock: time to give Oscar a drop of refreshment. With a slight sigh she picked him up from where he had been lying with some of her own reposeful placidity on a large clean napkin and then dropped one side of her magenta bikini top and produced a handsome expanse of bosom like a full-blown milky balloon. Into this Oscar buried himself with eager rapidity while Ma went on:

'Oh, talking about flirting and all that, I think we're going to have trouble with our Primrose.'

Primrose was eleven: even Pop, very faintly surprised, thought that was a bit dodgy.

'Trouble? How?'

'In love. Bad.'

Pop said he'd go to Jericho. In love? How was that?

101

'How?' Ma said. 'What do you mean, how? Naturally, that's how. Developing early, that's how. Like I did.'

Ah! well, Pop said, that was different. That was the right spirit. Nothing like starting young. Who was it? Not some French boy?

'Two,' Ma said.

Pop, laughing good-naturedly, remarked that he supposed there was safety in numbers, to which Ma firmly shook her head.

'That's just it. Can't sleep at night. She's trying to give one of 'em up and can't decide which one it's got to be.'

'Thought you said it was a good thing?' Pop said.

'Said what was a good thing?'

Pop, feeling himself to be rather sharp, laughed again.

'Variety.'

Instead of laughing in reply Ma regarded him with something like severity over the top of little Oscar's bald dumpling of a head.

'Sometimes I'm surprised at you, Sid Larkin,' she said. It was always a bit of a bad sign when she called him Sid Larkin. 'It's a very tricky age. You'll have to be careful what you say to her.'

'Me?' Pop said. 'Haven't said a word.'

Ma, deftly shifting little Oscar from one side of her bosom to the other, looked at him for some seconds before answering, this time with a glance more mysterious than severe, so that he was almost afraid she was going to call him Sid Larkin again. That would have been a bit much. She only did it once or twice a year — so's he'd

102

know it really meant something when she did.

'No,' she said darkly, 'you haven't. But you will.'

'Oh?' he said. 'When?'

'When the time comes,' Ma said blandly, 'when the time comes.'

Ma had him properly guessing now. He couldn't rumble her at all. There was something behind that Sid Larkin touch, he thought, and he was still trying to fathom what it was when Ma, in her habitually unruffled way, abruptly changed the subject by saying:

'Going back to Charley. I think a walk would do him more good. He sits on this beach too long. He's moping. Take him down to the harbour and have a drink with one of your fishermen friends. Didn't you say you had another deal cooking?'

That was right, Pop said. He had. He'd got the Froggy skipper interested in a hundred cases of that tinned gherkins in vinegar that he hadn't been able to hock to anybody else up to now. It would show about three hundred per cent if it came off. Nothing very big: but it would help to keep the pot boiling.

'Good idea,' he said.

He put one finger into his mouth and with a sudden piercing whistle, shrill as diamond on glass, startled the entire *plage* into thinking a train was coming. Mr Charlton, who was idly picking up shells and trying not to notice the antics of the god-like young Frenchmen prancing all about him, recognized the sign at once and came strolling over.

103

'Put your top hat on, Charley old man,' Pop said. 'I'm taking you down to the harbour for a wet. Fit?'

Charley said he was fit and called a few words of explanation to Mariette, who had discarded her bikini for a remarkable strapless sun suit in brilliant cinnamon with a boned front that uplifted and enlarged her bust to a sumptuous and thrilling degree.

The balls would be floating over any moment now, Charley thought, and he wondered suddenly if he had the courage to leave her there. She looked maddeningly beautiful, as she always did when sulky. Today she was all steamy voluptuousness, lying there languidly pouting in the warm morning sun, and he actually called:

'You're really absolutely sure you don't mind if I go?'

Mariette made no sign. It was Ma who shook her head. Pop was, after all, right about Charley's technique. There really were some serious gaps in it. He really ought to use his loaf sometimes.

'Darling!' he called.

'Yes?' Mariette said.

'You honestly don't mind?'

'Have a good time. Don't get drunk,' she said.

Probably not a bad idea, Pop mused as he and Charley walked along the harbour walls, watching the Breton fishing crews brewing buckets of fish and potatoes into one big steaming stew and loading red wine on to the decks by the dozen crates. It gave Pop great pleasure to watch all this and to gaze at the many furled copper umbrellas bright in the mid-morning sun above the crowded blue hulls.

'Don't see old Brisson about,' he said. 'Anyway we'll have a snifter at the Chat Noir. He'll be along.'

As he and Charley chose a pavement table at the café on the harbour's edge, Pop got the sudden idea that the occasion was one when they might try something a little special. It was too early for wine. It made him sleepy. And he was fed up with the eternal Dubonnet, Pernod, and Cinzano. What did Charley think about a real drink? Red Bull or something of that sort?

'First class idea, Pop,' Mr Charlton said. 'Absolutely first class.'

Pop, slightly astonished at the strenuous vehemence of Charley's tone, gave him a sharp glance of inquiry which he didn't bother to answer.

Charley was feeling a private need for a strong pick-me-up. It depressed him increasingly each time he thought of the young French gods, their stupid great balls, and Mariette sunning herself in her sumptuous cinnamon.

'Rattling good idea,' he said. 'I've been waiting for somebody to ask me that one.'

As Pop was about to call '*Garçon!*' and begin an explanation as to how to mix the Red Bulls he saw Captain Brisson arrive. Pop always called him Captain. Huge, florid, and purple, he looked very much like a large bulldog with heart disease.

Charley, having been introduced, suddenly took off his spectacles and started polishing

105

them madly. Pop, unaware of what made him do this, called to the waiter and at the same time started to explain to the Captain about the Red Bulls and did he want one?

'Plizz, what name? Red Bull, you say?'

'Red Bull. It's a self-propeller!' Mr Charlton said. 'A blinder!'

'Plizz?'

The Captain, like Pop, looked positively startled at the sudden vehemence of the small Englishman who, momentarily without his spectacles, looked so harmless, odd, and short-sighted.

'My son-in-law,' Pop said, as if this explained everything.

Mr Charlton rammed his spectacles back on his nose and in rapid French explained the composition of the cocktail that, only a year before, had knocked him flat. He was stronger now. He could take a dozen.

'Good,' Captain Brisson said, presently tasting the Red Bull, which Charley had had the forethought to order double. 'Good. I like. Good at sea.'

Searching stabs of raw alcohol inspired Charley to fresh, almost rapturous enthusiasm for the virtues of the cocktail.

'Propel the whole ruddy boat,' he said. 'Nothing like it. Absolute blinder. *Santé.*'

'*Santé,*' Captain Brisson said.

'Cheers!' Pop said. '*Santé.*'

'Cheers,' the Captain said.

'*Santé,*' Charley said. 'Down the hatch.'

He already thought, as Pop and Captain

Brisson sat discussing the question of sliced gherkins in vinegar, that he felt a great deal better. Pop was feeling pleased with himself too. The Captain had made a very reasonable offer for the hundred cases and the deal was now completed except for the formality of a little paper.

Since Pop was incapable of writing his name and the Captain incapable of writing English it devolved on Mr Charlton to draw up a sort of invoice, agreeing price and quantity. For some reason he chose to do this in pencil. He couldn't think why, since he had a perfectly good pen in his pocket, except perhaps that the pencil needed sharpening and that the short rapid strokes of his penknife gave him the same nervous outlet for his emotions as the mad polishing of his spectacles.

'I am content,' the Captain said. His signature and Pop's cross, binding nobody and nothing at all, were added to Mr Charlton's document, which the Frenchman kept. Pop never kept records. It was all in his head. 'I sank you.'

After this the Captain and Pop shook hands. Then Pop knocked his Red Bull straight back, declaring that the proceedings called for another drink to which Charley added a kind of vehement amen.

'You bet!' he said.

'Plizz,' the Captain said. 'I like to pay.'

'Rhubarb!' Charley said. 'This one's on me!'

After the second Red Bull he began to feel that the contemptuous memory of the young French gods and their stupid idiotic balls and still stupider prancings no longer disturbed him quite so much. He started to see the harbour through a viscous, rosy cloud.

Now and then he sharpened the pencil madly again and then, after a third Red Bull, actually started to sharpen it at the other end. About this time Captain Brisson said he ought to be going back to his boat and Pop said they ought to be going too.

'Rhubarb!' Charley said loudly. 'Hell's bells. We only just got here.'

'Please excuse,' the Captain said.

'Rhubarb!' Charley said again. 'I thought the French were drinkers.'

The Captain again protested that he had to get back to his ship and Pop said very well, that was all right, and he hoped he'd see him soon. Perhaps in England?

'In England, yes,' the Captain said. 'I come soon. When teeth are ready.'

'What teeth?' Charley snapped.

Without embarrassment and with a certain touch of pride the captain slipped from his mouth what he explained to Pop and Charley were his temporary set of dentures. The new ones, he assured them, would be ready in a month or so: in England.

'National Elf lark,' Pop reminded Charley.

'My mate,' the Captain said, 'he have new wooden leg. Also it is true you can have cognac sometimes? *Oui?*'

'There's the National Elf lark for you. Charley old man,' Pop said. 'Free for all. Even the Froggies. Wooden legs an' all.'

'Rhubarb to the National Health lark!' said Charley aggressively, 'and double rhubarb to the Froggies!'

As if detecting in this a certain note of ill-concealed hostility Captain Brisson, whose face had now broken out in a rash of red and purple blotches, shook hands all over again with Pop and Charley, at the same time forgetting to put his teeth back. It was only when he had gone some yards along the quayside that he remembered the omission and slapped them back into his mouth with a blow so sharp that it knocked him off keel, making him stagger.

Soon after he had disappeared Pop was about to say for a second time that he and Charley ought to be going too when he saw across the street a figure waving to him with a white and chocolate scarf.

He did not need to hear the fluted call of 'Darling!' that followed it to know that this was Angela Snow. She was dressed in trim pure white shorts and a coffee coloured linen blouse and white open sandals in which her bare painted toe-nails glistened like rows of cherries. With her was a girl in a pea-green cable-stitch sweater and a skirt of indeterminate colour that might have once been mustard. Much washing had turned it to an unpleasant shade of mongrel ochre, rather like that of a mangel-wurzel.

'This', said Angela Snow, 'is my sister. Iris.'

Pop and Charley rose to shake hands, Charley unsteadily.

'Good. Splendid,' Charley said. 'Just in time for a snifter.'

'Darlings!' Angela Snow said. 'My tongue's hanging out.'

Iris said nothing but 'Howdedo'. She was a solid, shortish blonde of rising thirty with a skin as hard as marble and more or less the colour of an acid drop. Her eyes were almost lashless; the complete absence of eyebrows made her face actually seem broader than it was, as well as giving it a look of completely bloodless astonishment. Her hair was cut in a roughish home-made bob and she had small white ankle socks of exactly the kind that French girls wear.

Charley demanded of the two girls what would it be and presently Angela Snow was drinking Pernod and her sister a small bottle of Perrier with ice. Charley and Pop decided at the same time that this was as good a moment as any to have a fourth Red Bull and while this was being mixed Pop reminded Angela Snow of her luncheon promise and when was she coming?

'Whenever you say, dear boy. At the given moment I shall be there.'

'Tomorrow?'

'Tomorrow, darling, as ever is. Bless you.'

'And your sister,' Pop said, giving Iris a rich perky look that would have melted Mademoiselle Dupont to tears but that had on Angela Snow's sister only the effect of heightening her appearance of bloodless surprise, 'would she care to join us too?'

'I'm sure she'd adore to.'

'Impossible,' Iris said. 'I go to Guimiliau to see the Calvary and then the ossuary at — '

The word ossuary startled Pop so much that

he gave a sort of frog-croak into his Red Bull, which had just arrived. He had as sharp an ear as ever for strange new words but this one had him floored.

'What', he said, 'is an ossuary? Sounds *très snob.*'

'Bone-house,' Angela Snow said.

'Same to you,' Pop said.

'Scream!' she said and everyone, with the solid exception of Iris, roared with laughter.

Even before the arrival of the fourth Red Bull Charley was feeling great. The bit about the ossuary served merely to put him into louder, cheerier, more pugnacious mood.

'Rhubarb!' he said to Iris Snow. 'Of course you can come. It's *langoustine* day tomorrow. Have them every Thursday. Don't you adore *langoustines?*'

Iris, who thought eating had much in common with the other deadly sins and consequently existed mostly on dry toast, cheese biscuits, and anchovy paste, had no word of answer.

'You see she visits somewhere different every day,' Angela Snow said in explanation. 'Ah! the calvaries and the crosses, the dolmens and the menhirs, the *allées couvertes* and the tumuli — Iris has to see them all.'

Pop sat open-mouthed before what he thought was the oddest female he had ever seen in his life but was saved from pondering over her too long by a sudden, almost pugnacious question from Charley.

'And how', he demanded of Iris, 'do you travel, Miss Snow? By car or what?'

111

Iris permitted herself the astonishing luxury of uttering fifty-six words all at once, speaking with measured solemnity.

'I think walking is the only true and right way of seeing these things. Walking leads to contemplation, contemplation to mood, and mood to meditation, so that when you get there you are one with the place you're visiting. So I walk to all the nearest ones and go to all the distant ones by train.'

'By train?' Charley said. 'What train? Not by any chance that *little* train?'

'Of course. What else? Whenever and as often as its — '

'My God!' Charley gave a positive shout of delighted triumph and gazed at Iris Snow with alcoholic rapture, as to a kindred spirit. 'She knows my little train! Hear that, Pop? She knows my little train!'

Pop, who thought something must have got into Charley — he'd start spouting Shakespeare or that feller Keats any moment now, he thought — could only stare at Angela Snow, who gave him a split-second sporting wink, without the trace of a smile, in reply. He was too astonished even to wink back again.

'That train,' Charley kept saying. 'That little train. You remember, Pop, how that was the first thing that brought it all back again?'

Brought all what back again? Pop wanted to know.

'Me. This. Everything. All that time. All those years. The whole ruddy shooting match.'

No doubt about it, Pop thought, Charley was

112

as drunk as a newt. Pickled. Something had got into him. It reminded him of the time he had first met him and how Mariette had had to lend him pyjamas and put him to bed. There was the same raving, rhapsodic light in his eyes.

'Chuffing away over the heather!' Charley said. He had started to wave his arms about in ecstatic recollection. 'Chuffing away for miles. I remember once — where was it? St Pol de Léon — no, not there. Somewhere else. No. Has St Pol de Léon two cathedrals?'

Without knowing it, and for no sane reason at all, Charley had begun to sharpen his pencil again.

'You might almost say it has,' Iris Snow said. 'There's the cathedral itself, and then of course there's the *Chapelle du Creizker*. Much, much more magnificent.'

'It was there!' Charley said with a rhapsodic jolt in his voice. 'It was there!'

What was? Pop wanted to know.

'Charley's got a spider on the end of his nose,' said Angela Snow, who loved practical jokes and who was dying to get the subject changed, since relics, saints, and pardons were her sister's food and drink, day and night. 'I can see it dangling.'

Charley did nothing about the supposed teasing spider except to snatch vaguely at the air immediately in front of him and then start stirring his Red Bull madly with his pencil, as if it were a cup of tea.

'First time I ever really saw the world,' he said. 'Consciously, I mean. Consciously. From that tower you can see — '

'Seventy other towers,' Iris said. 'Of course on a clear day.'

'Never forget,' Charley said. 'God, you talk about 'a wild surmise — silent upon a peak in Darien' — '

'Charley's off,' Pop said. 'More Shakespeare.'

'Keats!' Charley shouted. 'Keats!'

'Same thing,' Pop said.

'Whenever I go there again,' Iris Snow said, 'I shall think of you.'

'Do,' Charley said, 'do,' and started to sharpen his pencil madly again. 'Think of me!'

Suddenly he was on top of the tower again, on top of the world. Everything was splendidly revelatory and wonderful. His insides felt rich with Red Bull. His veins were a jumble of wires that sang like harp-strings. He heard himself order a fifth Red Bull in a voice that echoed inside his head as a cry might have done through one of the sepulchral *allées couvertes* that Iris found so fascinating.

Drinking it, he was aware that his intestines were on fire and he suddenly gave a belch of rude immoderation.

Magnifique, he kept telling Iris Snow. *Magnifique*. Rhubarb! And he didn't care a damn for any of the bastards. Did she?

Whether it had anything to do with this robustly repeated inquiry he never knew but suddenly he came to a vague realization that neither Angela Snow nor her sister were there any longer.

'Where have the Snows gone?' he said. 'Melted?' Jolly good joke, he thought. *Magnifique*. 'Snows all melted?'

114

Some time later he was dimly aware of walking back to the *plage* with Pop, still madly sharpening his pencil and still saying he didn't care a damn for the bastards, whoever they were.

'All Froggies are alike,' he was saying as they reached the *plage*. 'Eh, Pop? No guts. No Red Bull. No red blood. Eh? Can't take it, eh?'

Without waiting for an answer he made a sudden spasmodic leap on to the sand, landing midway between Ma, who was giving further refreshment to Oscar, and Mariette who, sumptuous in fiery cinnamon in the noon sun, was flirting madly with a muscular Frenchman bronzed as evenly all over as if every inch of colour had been painted on.

Charley at once uttered a queer cry, half in warning, half in anger, and rushed across the sand, seawards, as if about to drown himself. The *plage*, it seemed to him, was full of balls. They were floating everywhere, maddening him as they had never done before.

Suddenly he started charging hither and thither with the violence of a demented buffalo. He was attacking balls everywhere as if they were monsters, stabbing at them with his open pen-knife, making them burst.

One of several loud reports startled a French woman into a scream and another startled Ma in the act of giving Oscar the other side. One ball as vivid a shade of mustard as Iris Snow's skirt had once been was floating in the water. Charley charged it with a dive, leaving it swimming on the surface of the waves like a deflated and forgotten tooth-bag.

Pop, who didn't know what to make of it all, stared blankly at Charley giving the death blow to a big pink and purple ball that went up with a crack like a Roman Candle, merely thinking that perhaps they'd better lay off Red Bulls for a bit, in case Charley got violent sometime. They didn't suit everybody, especially on an empty stomach.

Less than a minute later he was shaken out of this complacency by the sight of Charley rushing back with puffing frenzy across the sand, every ball now triumphantly punctured, to where Mariette, luxuriously lying on her back under the gaze of an admiring Frenchman who stood with hands on his knees, was testing the truth of Ma's shrewd observations on variety.

In full flight, Charley kicked the startled Frenchman twice up the backside. He was, however, less startled than Pop, who suddenly heard Charley, as he lugged an astonished Mariette to her feet, ripping out the challenging words:

'And tomorrow you'll come on the little train! Hear that? You'll come with me on the little train!'

In bed that night, in the quiet of darkness, Pop was still trying to work out this violent episode for himself.

'So that', he said, 'was what all the hoo-ha was about. That little train. Don't get it, Ma. Do you?'

Ma said of course she got it. It was as plain as a pikestaff.

'How? Don't get it,' he said.

'Charley wanted to go on the little train and

116

Mariette didn't. That's all.'

Lot of fuss for nothing Pop thought. All over a little thing like that. All over a train.

'Not at all,' Ma said. 'It's always the little things. That train means a lot to Charley.'

Pop said he thought it seemed like it too.

'It's connected with something in him,' Ma said. 'In his childhood.'

'Never!' Pop said. 'Really?' For crying out gently.

'It stands for something he's lost. Or else something he's never had. Not sure which.'

Pop said he shouldn't think so either. Charley would have to take more water with it, that was all.

'It's psychology,' Ma said. 'You hear a lot about it on telly.'

Wonderful thing, Pop remarked, telly. He missed it on holiday. It learnt you something all the time. Every day. Ma said she agreed. She missed the *Mirror* too. Without it she never knew what her stars foretold and that made it awkward somehow.

At last, lying under the lee of Ma's huge mountain of a body, Pop found himself going back over the day and in the course of doing so remembered something else he thought remarkable.

'Heard a word today, though, Ma,' he said, 'I've never even heard on telly yet. And I'll bet you never have either.'

Oh, and what word was that? Ma wanted to know.

'Ossuary.'

And whatever in the world did that mean?

'Bone-house to you,' Pop told her.

'Do you mind?' Ma said and kicked him hard under the bedclothes. 'Whatever next? You'll have the twins picking it up in no time.'

'Sorry, Ma,' Pop said. '*Dormez bien*. Sleep well.'

'Sleep well, my foot,' Ma said and gave her handsome head a swift twist on the pillow, so that she was lying full face to him. 'What makes you think I'm all that tired?'

Pop said he couldn't think and immediately set to work to demonstrate that he wasn't all that tired either.

7

But it was always Ma, in her unruffled way, who shrewdly remembered the best and most important things and it was she who, next morning after breakfast, called Pop's attention to an event a week ahead.

'You know', she said, 'what it is next Thursday?'

Pop didn't; except that they were going home.

'That's Friday,' Ma said. 'Thursday the 29th I mean.'

Pop said he couldn't think what the twenty-ninth meant at all; he only knew that the month at St Pierre le Port seemed to have gone like the wind. He could hardly believe that soon they were going home.

'Mariette and Charley,' Ma said. 'Their wedding anniversary.'

'Completely forgot,' Pop said.

'Forgot, my foot,' Ma said slyly. 'The trouble is you don't get much practice with wedding anniversaries, do you?'

Pop confessed that this was quite true but nevertheless suggested darkly that he and Ma made up for it in other ways.

'Good thing too,' Ma said. 'Anyway, I thought we ought to give them a party.'

Perfick idea, Pop said. Jolly fine idea. Perfick. Très snob.

'I thought we could ask Angela Snow and her

sister and perhaps Mademoiselle Dupont. How does that strike you?'

Pop said that nothing could have struck him better. It was just the job. Mariette would be thrilled too.

'By the way,' Ma said, 'what's Angela Snow's sister like? If she's anything like her we'll have a high old party.'

She wasn't, Pop said.

'Oh?' Ma said. 'What's she like then?'

Pop found it difficult to say. He could find no handy word to describe Iris Snow with any sort of accuracy. He thought hard for some moments and then said:

'All I know is she wears false boosies and she's very pale.'

What a shame, Ma said. She was very sorry about that. She always pitied girls who had to wear those things. Good boosies were a girl's crowning glory, as you could see from all the advertisements there were about them everywhere nowadays.

Pop heartily agreed and invited Ma to consider our Mariette for instance, which in turn made him remark that he was glad to see that she and Charley were well on hooks again.

'Like love-birds,' Ma said. 'We must give them a good time on Thursday. The tops.'

Best party they could think up, Pop said. What did Ma suggest?

'Well,' Ma said, 'I tell you what I thought. I thought that as we've got Angela Snow coming to lunch today we'd discuss it all then. We can get Mademoiselle Dupont in over coffee and all talk about what we're going to eat and drink and so on. Have a proper laid-out menu and the table decorated and all that. How's that strike you?'

Again Pop thought it struck him very well. They could get all the wines ordered too and he would try to think up some special sort of cocktail. The expense could be damned; the gherkins and the cucumber in vinegar lark would take care of that.

'Good,' Ma said. 'Now perhaps we'll get some real food.'

At lunch, before Mademoiselle Dupont joined them for coffee, a small but quite unprecedented incident took place: in Pop's experience anyway. The day was coolish, with a touch of that bristling westerly wind that could blow fine sand into every corner and crevice like chaff from a thresher. Even Angela Snow had put on a thick red sweater and Pop noticed that in spite of it she shuddered as she first sat down.

'Let's give the vin rosy a rest, shall we, Ma?' Pop said. 'Have something a bit more warming today.'

Just what she felt like, Ma said. Pop must choose a good one.

'Sky's the limit,' Pop said, and with infinite charm turned to Angela Snow and suggested that she should make the choice.

The customary Thursday *langoustines* not having arrived because the sea had been too rough it presently turned out that for lunch there was *potage du jour* and *omelette au fromage* followed by *côtes de porc grillées* with *haricots verts*.

'In that case burgundy,' Angela Snow said.

'A good one, mind, the real McCoy,' Pop said. 'No half larks. The best.'

Angela Snow said she thought in that case that the Chambolle Musigny '47 couldn't be bettered.

'Fire away,' Pop said. 'Make it two bottles.'

A waitress finally brought the wine in a basket cradle. A lot of dust covered the bottle and this, to Pop, was a sure sign of something good. The waitress then pulled the cork and poured out a little of the wine for Pop to taste but Pop was quick to say:

'No, no. Angela. Angela must taste it.'

She did.

'Corked,' she said firmly. 'No doubt about it. Must go back.'

A curious suspended hush settled on the table, broken only after some seconds by Primrose asking in a piping voice:

'What's corked, Pop?'

Pop didn't know; he hadn't the remotest idea what corked was. Obviously this wine lark was a bit dodgy, he thought, and privately decided he must go into it a bit more closely. There were things he didn't know.

'Of course it can happen any time, anywhere,' Angela Snow said. 'It's nobody's fault. It's one of those things.'

Pop said he was relieved to hear it and was on the verge of saying that 'corked' might not be a bad word to describe Iris Snow when he thought better of it and decided not to, in case Ma should somehow misunderstand.

The direct result of all this was that when

coffee was brought Mademoiselle Dupont came to the table in more than usually nervous, apologetic mood. She apologized several times for the unfortunate incident of the Chambolle Musigny. Aware though she was of the ease with which it could happen at any time, anywhere, even to the best of wines, she would nevertheless have rather cut off her right hand than it should happen to milord Larkin and his family.

At the word milord Angela Snow was astounded into a silence from which she hadn't recovered by the time Ma was suggesting to an equally astonished Mademoiselle Dupont that the party wouldn't be complete if the children didn't have custard and jelly for afters.

Meanwhile the coffee filters had to be attacked. Pop always dealt with his, though never very successfully, by giving it a number of smart hostile slaps with the flat of his hand. Mostly these produced no visible result whatever. Charley's method was more simple. He merely pressed the top down hard and invariably spilt what coffee there was all over the place.

On the other hand Mademoiselle Dupont seemed lucky enough to be blessed with a special sort of filter, for while everyone else was struggling messily to coax a few black drops of liquid into the cups she was sipping away with alacrity, trying to calm her nerves.

'First, to decide how many people.'

Ma counted up the heads.

'Not counting Oscar and I think he's a bit young, don't you?' she said, 'I think there'll be a round dozen. That includes you', she said to

Angela Snow, 'and your sister. And,' she said to Mademoiselle Dupont, 'you too.'

Mademoiselle Dupont's pale olive face at once started flushing. She was most flattered, most honoured, but really it couldn't be. Her French and English began to mix themselves hopelessly, as always at times when she was excessively nervous, and she could only blurt out that it was *très difficile, impossible*, quite *impossible*. There would be so much *travail* and Alphonse would need much watching.

'Who's Alphonse?' Pop said.

'He is the *chef*. He is not an easy man.'

Drinks, Ma thought. She knew. Nearly all cooks drank. Like fishes, too, though perhaps you couldn't blame them.

'Alphonse will be looked after,' said Pop, who had by now abandoned the struggle with the coffee filter and had lit up one of his best Havanas. 'The main thing is the grub. Kids,' he said to Charley and Mariette, 'what do you fancy to start with?'

Mariette said she's been trying to think but it was Mr Charlton, always so bang on the target in these things, who made the happy suggestion that he thought they ought to begin with *melon au porto*.

'With that', he pointed out, 'you eat and get a drink at the same time.'

It was cordially agreed by everyone, especially Pop, that *melon au porto* sounded marvellous. Mademoiselle Dupont thought so too, saying several times over that she thought she could get the lovely, small *charentais* melons, which were

124

the best, if she tried hard.

'And then may I suggest *filets de sole aux truffes?*'

'Troof, troof!' the twins started saying. 'Troof! Troof!'

'Quiet!' Pop thundered and the twins stopped as if throttled.

'How do you feel about that, Mariette?' Ma said. 'Wouldn't rather have lobster?'

'How is the *filet de sole* composed?' Charley said.

The rather grand word 'composed' seemed to flatter Mademoiselle Dupont so greatly that she started to describe the contents of the dish with both verve and tenderness.

'*Vin blanc*, white wine, butter, *les truffes*, and *quelques autres choses très délicieuses* — '

'Sounds just the job,' Pop said. 'Chips with it?'

Mademoiselle Dupont recoiled from the suggestion of chips with silence, not really understanding exactly what it meant. The milord was a comic man sometimes.

Eventually everyone agreed that the *filet de sole aux truffes* didn't sound too bad at all, though Pop was privately disappointed that there was no further mention of chips. You always had chips with fish. What was wrong?

'And now as to meat? Or should it possibly be chicken? Or perhaps some other bird?'

Suddenly, while everyone was trying to concentrate on the problems of this, the main course, Victoria bit Zinnia sharply on the ear. Nobody took much notice of this except Petunia, who threw at Victoria a piece of *omelette au fromage* she hadn't been able to eat because it tasted of soapsuds. In a second all three girls were crying and Ma was saying seriously, as if there wasn't a ghost of sound to be heard:

'I as good as told you so.'

'Quiet!' Pop thundered for the second time in ten minutes and there was instant silence at the table, so that Ma remarked with pride, as she so often did, that Pop had them at a word.

The effect of this was to impress Mademoiselle Dupont tremendously. The English milord was obviously a most masterful person. A man clearly born to command. You could tell these born, masterful, commanding aristocrats fifty kilometrès away.

This was the season for *perdrix*, she was saying suddenly. There were now beautiful young *perdrix*. What was the English word? — partridge? Shouldn't they therefore select partridge? — *perdrix*, perhaps, *à la mode d'ici?*

It suddenly occurred to Pop that he had heard these ominous words somewhere before. They struck a faint and unpleasant chord in his mind. And in a flash he remembered the pregnant sausage-rolls with steam coming out of their ends.

Partridges — no — he said, he didn't think so. No *à la mode d'ici.*

'If it's all right with Charley and Mariette,' he said, 'I know what I want and what I should like to have.'

'Go on. Say it,' Ma said. 'I know.'

'Roast beef and Yorkshire.'

'Biff! Biff!' the twins started saying but this

126

time a single look was enough to silence them.

'Can't wait,' Charley said.

'Lovely!' Mariette said. 'Couldn't be anything better. Oh! Pop, you always have the sweetest ideas.'

Pop, feeling rather flattered by this, gave one of his perkiest, richest smiles at Mademoiselle Dupont, who responded confusedly by saying:

'*Rosbif* of course. That we can arrange. But what else was this you said? This Jorkshire?'

Pop started to explain that this was, in his opinion, a pudding that had no equal. It was about the best in the world.

'I see,' Mademoiselle Dupont said. 'It is merely a question of whether Alphonse can make it. I doubt it very much.'

'Then Ma can make it for him,' Pop said.

Mademoiselle Dupont professed to be instantly and completely horrified. It was quite out of the question. It was unthinkable that a stranger should go into the kitchen, still less teach Alphonse how to make strange dishes. It would only offend him. He was at the best of times a temperamental man and sometimes, after drink, ran about with carving knives.

'Fetch Alphonse,' Pop said. 'I daresay he wouldn't say no to a brandy. I want one too.'

Mademoiselle Dupont now fluffed over her coffee, which she had allowed to get quite cold. Alphonse also, she recalled, but not aloud, had a mistress in Morlaix and two in Brest. He visited the three of them in rotation and they too sometimes had strange effects on his stability.

Alphonse, duly called in from the kitchen, didn't

say no to a brandy. He was a man of stocky proportions, inclined to be portly, with very black hair parted down the middle with millimetrical exactitude and polished with a great deal of violet brilliantine. His eyes were protuberant but handsome and in the space of three seconds from first entering the *salle à manger* he managed to give Ma, Angela Snow, and Mariette the quickest, most comprehensive once-over.

Since Alphonse spoke no English it was left to Mr Charlton, translating instructions from Ma, to explain the composition of what Mademoiselle Dupont called the *pouding à la Jorkshire*. These instructions, though simple in the extreme, were listened to by Alphonse with aloofness, not to say contempt, while he drank in the visionary beauty of Angela Snow, who had for a long time sat in a state of bemusement, not saying a word.

Suddenly Alphonse became unexpectedly voluble and first Mademoiselle Dupont and then Mr Charlton translated his words for Ma.

'He says if you will write it down on paper it shall be made as you wish. And is it the same as for *crêpes*?'

'Pancakes,' Mr Charlton explained.

'Exactly the same,' Ma said. 'Couldn't be more right.'

'*Ça va bien*,' Pop said. '*Merci beaucoup, Alphonse*.'

Alphonse said '*Merci, monsieur*' and immediately became suddenly voluble again. This time it was to offer the suggestion that the beef should be the *contre filet*, which Mademoiselle Dupont applauded as being absolutely right, quite excellent.

'And now what about afters?' Ma said.

'Ah!' Pop said smartly, picking it up in a flash. 'Les après.'

Alphonse looked witheringly about him for a second or two and then held a short conversation with Mademoiselle Dupont, who said:

'Alphonse is suggesting either crêpes Suzette for dessert or bombe surprise.'

It was at this moment that Angela Snow came out of her half dream to hear Ma insisting on jelly and custard for the children and to find herself being shamelessly and mentally undressed by Alphonse's over-large handsome eyes.

'I think myself the crêpes Suzette,' she said, staring straight through Alphonse. 'They'll keep him busier at the time.'

'That about settles it then,' Ma said.

'No it don't though,' Pop said. 'What about the cake? Got to have a cake. Midnight, champagne, and all that lark.'

'Oh! Pop, lovely!' Mariette said and suddenly ran round the table in one of her moments of spontaneous delight to kiss Pop with luscious gratitude. 'Cake and champagne — it's like being married all over again!'

'Second honeymoon, Charley, second honeymoon,' Pop said, hoping the cheerful pointed words wouldn't be lost on him. 'Second honeymoon.'

Charley, using his loaf, looked as if he understood. Then Mademoiselle Dupont said Alphonse would be most honoured to make the cake. And if there were any other things, any other thoughts — suddenly a great sense of excitement ran through her, as if the party were really her own, and she ended by half-running out of the *salle à manger* into the Bureau in another fluff, repeating half in French, half in English, a few uncertain sentences which nobody could understand.

For another half hour, while Charley, Mariette, and the children went to the *plage* and Pop for a gentle snooze on the bed, Ma and Angela Snow sat outside on the terrace, drinking coffee. By this time the sun had appeared but the air was quite autumnal. Already at the end of the terrace a few leaves of the plane trees pollarded to give shade in hot weather were turning yellow and even falling to the ground. The bead-like strings of coloured lights, shattered by storm and still unrepaired, gave the trees an air of premature shabbiness that was like a small herald of winter. It was all too true, as Mademoiselle Dupont had remarked to Ma only that morning after breakfast, that the season was coming to its end. The guests were departing. Soon the hotel would be empty. The French had no taste for the sea when October began and in another week or two the little *plage* would be wrapped away for winter.

Presently Angela Snow was saying how much she was looking forward to the party and what a lot you missed by not being married: the anniversaries and that sort of thing.

'Suppose you do,' Ma said. She'd never really thought of it.

'I'll have to settle down myself I suppose one of these days,' Angela Snow said.

'Oh?' Ma said. 'Why?'

She didn't mind a scrap everyone knowing

that she and Pop weren't married — most took it for granted they were and anyway it looked the same, even if it wasn't — and she remained quite unperturbed and unsurprised when Angela Snow, who liked to be frank in everything, said in an off-hand way:

'Don't you ever think of marrying Pop?'

Ma threw back her dark handsome head and roared with laughter.

'What?' she said, 'and give him a chance to leave me?'

'Scream,' Angela Snow said. 'Suppose he might at that.'

'Off like a hare.'

Angela laughed so much over her filtered half-cold coffee that she spilt most of it into the saucer. It was undrinkable anyway: as she had long since discovered filtered coffee always was. But she nevertheless supposed the French would always cling to it, just as the Scots did to herring and oatmeal.

'Well, must go,' she said. 'Must see what the adventurous Iris has been up to. Let me know if ever he does.'

Ma laughed in her friendliest fashion.

'Who? Pop? I'll send you a wire. That'll give you a bit of a start on Mademoiselle Dupont.'

'Oh! is she in the hunt too?'

Ma said she was afraid so. She'd be in a whale of a tizzy by the time that party was over.

'And not the only one.'

Graceful and elegant, Angela Snow stooped to kiss Ma a sporting goodbye, telling her at the same time to give Pop her best love, which Ma warmly promised to do, with knobs of brass and tinkling cymbals, as Pop himself was so fond of saying sometimes.

'God bless,' Angela said. 'Have to fix a hair-do somehow before that party. For two pins I'd have my blasted face lifted as well.'

'Where to?' Ma said, laughing again. 'You keep it as it is. Pop'd never forgive you.'

Angela Snow went back into the hotel on the pretext of telephoning a hairdresser but in reality on the offchance of running into Pop as he came downstairs. But the lounge, the reception desk, and the stairs were all deserted and she suddenly realized with unpleasantness that she might run into Alphonse instead. She didn't care for Alphonse. The process of being mentally undressed by strange men had never amused her. Nor, for some reason, did she like men who parted their hair down the middle. But now and then she couldn't help wondering what the virginal Iris would make of those too large, too handsome eyes.

'Did Mademoiselle wish for something please?'

It was Mademoiselle Dupont who came at length to the door of the Bureau and called the words. In reply Angela Snow said she was wondering about a hairdresser and was there one she could go to in the town?

'There is nothing exciting here. Nothing soigné. One must go to Morlaix or Brest.'

'Oh? Then I might go to Brest.'

'Phillippe: that is the name.'

'Phillippe,' Angela Snow said. 'Do you go there?'

'I regret not often. I can't afford it.'

'No? Not even for the party?'

Mademoiselle Dupont, who had been torn all day by the question of whether to have a hair-do or a new corset for the party and had almost decided on the corset, could only gaze in silence at Angela Snow's exquisitely smooth aristocratic yellow hair and wish that her own were like it, so that such difficult dilemmas and choices never arose.

'Got to make the party a success you know,' Angela Snow said.

'I think that Milord Larkin', Mademoiselle Dupont said rather loftily, 'will see to that. He has the *flair*.'

Drawn up sharply by the second mention of the word milord that day, Angela Snow had no time to make any sort of comment before Mademoiselle Dupont fluffed again and said:

'I am right in thinking that? Yes? He is a milord?'

'Down to the ankles,' Angela Snow said. 'And like every Englishman he's sure his home is his castle.'

At the mention of the word castle Mademoiselle Dupont was unable to speak. A castle — a *château*. There was something overpowering, *très formidable*, about the word castle.

'You must ask him to tell you about it,' Angela Snow said.

'I will ask that,' Mademoiselle Dupont said quietly.

After Angela Snow had departed Mademoiselle Dupont went upstairs. In her room she took off her dress, as she did every afternoon, and lay down on the bed. Like Angela Snow she had hoped for the chance of running into Pop on the stairs but nothing had happened and she lay for an hour alone and in silence, thinking largely of milord Larkin, the castle, and how altogether surprising the English were, but also of the entrancements of marriage and a lot of other things. She remembered the occasion when Pop had caressed her, brief and idle though it had been, with a warm swift hand, and how he would for ever remember her bedroom when he caught the scent of *les muguets*.

At the end of it she decided there was nothing for it but to have her hair dressed at Phillippe's and buy the new corset too. After all, she thought in typical French fashion, the bill for the party would be a big one and she would be able to afford it out of that.

She would have her hair done in that Empire style that was now so fashionable and that she knew would give her the illusion of height she needed so much. The corset must be a black one, trimmed with lace in parma violet at top and bottom, and every time she thought of it she started trembling.

8

The evening of the party was warm and sultry, only the softest westerly wind ruffling the sea into small white pleats on the sand along the *plage*.

Dinner, Mademoiselle Dupont had suggested, should be at eight-thirty. This would give the only two French families remaining in the hotel time to finish their food in comfort before retiring to the lounge. She had herself superintended the laying of the one long table, decorating it with bright orange dahlias, dark red rose petals strewn about the cloth, and sprays of asparagus fern.

Pop, who entranced everybody by appearing in a biscuit-coloured light-weight suit and a yellow silk bow-tie with large cranberry spots on it and a handkerchief to match, spent most of the time between six and seven mixing punch in the bar, tasting it frequently to see if it was any good at all. He finally decided it was a bit of a snorter.

He had seen the recipe for punch in some magazine Ma had bought. It was known as Colonel Bramley's Punch and you could have it either hot or cold, Pop deciding that since the evening was so sultry he would make it cold. Plenty of ice was the form.

The main ingredients were rum, white wine, Curaçao, lemon, and sugar, but after the first mixing Pop decided that the flavour of rum was, if anything, rather too prominent. Not everybody liked rum. He added brandy. This brought out a certain heaviness in the mixture. It needed sharpening up a bit. He tried a tumbler of Kirsch for this and decided that it was exactly the right thing for giving the punch a subtler but at the same time more brittle tone. When the ice was added just before seven o'clock, when everybody was expected to arrive, he casually decided that another bottle of white wine and a second dash of brandy wouldn't do anybody any harm at all and these were added together with large slices of fresh orange and a scattering of cocktail cherries, which had the effect of making the whole thing look pretty, amusing, partyish, and at the same time quite innocuous.

Although Ma, Mariette, Charley, and the children came downstairs after seven o'clock and gathered in the bar, from which Mademoiselle Dupont had actually removed last year's heather and replaced it by bowls of dark purple asters, there was no sign of Angela Snow and her sister until a quarter to eight or of Mademoiselle Dupont until nearly forty minutes later.

Meanwhile the children drank Coca-cola and orange juice and the four grown-ups sampled the punch. Sometimes Ma allowed the children to sample the punch too and also sneak a slice of orange or a cherry out of it with their fingers so that they could have an extra suck.

'Good pick-me-up on a wash-day this, Pop,' she said. Just what she wanted. 'Wondered why you'd been so quiet since six o'clock.'

Ma was wearing a low-cut dress in deep

136

purple, much the colour of the asters, with a narrow mink stole. She was drenched in a new perfume called 'Kick' and was wearing a pearl and diamanté comb in one side of her hair and three handsome rows of pearls round her neck. Mariette was wearing a dress of stunning low-cut simplicity in burgundy velvet, effective in its sheer richness but also because there was so little of it, and a necklace of garnet and diamond that Pop had bought her in Brest for the anniversary.

Now and then Pop decided that the punch was going down rather too fast and added another harmless dash of rum, a little Kirsch, or a glass of brandy.

By a quarter to eight, when Angela and Iris Snow arrived, the character of the mixture had changed completely, though Pop, by adding orange and cherries again, kept it looking much the same. Ma thought that, if anything, it was much nicer now.

'Very more-ish,' she said and settled down to a fifth glass of it. 'And so cool.'

As soon as Angela Snow and her sister arrived Pop remarked how warm the evening was and was quick to press them to a cooling glass.

'Ingredients?' Angela Snow said as she tasted it. 'I think it's another of your blinders.'

Cheers, she went on to say, if it was. If not there was plenty of time.

'Women's magazine recipe. Practically teetotal,' Pop explained. 'It's actually the coolth that makes it what it is.'

Iris Snow, who liked Pop's word coolth, sipped happily.

Their lateness in arrival was, she explained, entirely due to her. She had been to see a calvary at St Thégonnec and had missed the train. She smiled with unusual readiness and apologized. Her hair looked less home-cut than usual, Pop thought, and the dark coffee-brown frock she was wearing, apart from the fact that in the haste of dressing she had evidently had some difficulty in balancing the two protuberances underneath it, so that one was much lower than the other, suited her quite well and was modestly attractive.

But it was Angela Snow's dress that had everyone wide-eyed in admiration. Pop thought it a corker. If she had a stitch on underneath it he would be more than surprised. The embroidered purity of its line, somehow accentuated by her long drop ear-rings, was even more fetching than its colour, a pale turquoise, and the fact that it fitted like a skin.

About eight o'clock M. Mollet crept in, mole-like as ever, as if out of hiding. He had been sent to say that Mademoiselle Dupont wouldn't be long; she had been delayed by complications of the kitchen.

She had in fact been delayed by complications of the new corset. It was rather tight and the zip was awkward. Twice she had run down for one of the chambermaids to come and help zip her up but they were all giving a hand in the kitchen and it was M. Mollet who at last came up to her room, to face the unparalleled embarrassment of finding Mademoiselle Dupont less than half-dressed, with a figure white as marble under a shining sheath of pure black and purple frills.

The experience left him not knowing whether he was going this way or that. It was then crowned by the sudden vision of the tall English girl in long ear-rings and pure turquoise and the disturbing fact that though she was fully dressed she actually seemed to have far fewer clothes on than Mademoiselle Dupont had in her bedroom. A cosmic explosion could hardly have shaken him more. A kind of low sea-sickness rocked through him and Pop gave him a glass of punch, which he accepted in a nervous daze, confident only, as Mademoiselle Dupont already was, that things in the hotel had never been quite like this before and never would be again.

Nobody took much notice of the self-effacing little figure in black coat and pin-stripe trousers and presently he crept out again, head held timidly down, so that he accidentally knocked against Pop, who was ladling out a third glass of punch for Charley.

'*Quel twirp*,' Pop said and there was laughter from everybody except Angela Snow, who suddenly realized that, for some unaccountable reason, she felt intensely sorry for the little reception clerk, who spent all his days burrowing between desk and bureau, for ever like a mole.

It was twenty-five minutes past eight before Mademoiselle Dupont entered the bar. This was a strange experience in itself, since she could recall no one having had a drink there since Liberation Day. In traditional French fashion she was wearing all black, with long pearl-drop ear-rings to give the illusion of that extra height she needed. Tonight she looked positively *chic* and was enveloped in a strong sensational cloud of lily-of-the-valley.

Pop, whose progress in French had been quite marked — always so quick to pick everything up, as Ma said — went straight over to her, clasped her by both hands and said:

'Mademoiselle! Enchantay!' as if he had been doing it all his life.

'Delayed in the kitchen, my foot,' Angela Snow thought and realized suddenly that she was madly, unreasonably jealous. It was quite unlike her.

'Fascinating tie,' she said and went over to finger Pop's large yellow and cranberry butterfly that made him look so dashing. 'French?'

'English,' Pop said.

'Has that air,' she said. 'The Froggies simply couldn't do it, dear boy.'

The word 'Froggies' made Mademoiselle Dupont bristle. She had begun the evening with nervous apprehension anyway, the complications of the kitchen being so great and those of the corset hardly less so. She felt all too conscious of the corset. She was sure it would make her itch before the night was gone.

'Drink up,' Pop said. 'Everybody have one more for the wagon train.'

Mademoiselle Dupont, sipping punch, deliberately turned her back on Angela Snow and asked to be told what this cool, charming liquid was.

'In *anglais*, punch,' Pop said.

'*Ah! le punch.*'

'*Spécialité de la maison Larkin*,' Pop said. 'Larkin Special. Goes down well, eh? *Très bon, n'est-ce pas?*'

'*Extraordinaire. Excellent,*' Mademoiselle Dupont said and then remembered how, in books about England, one always read of gentlemen drinking *le punch*. It was like tea and fog: it was part of the true English scene. Everyone knew, of course, that England was perpetually shrouded in fog, that the sun hardly ever shone there and that no one ever, or hardly ever, drank anything but tea. But now she had recalled *le punch*. Undoubtedly it was an aristocratic thing.

She now suggested that they might, at any time, go in to dinner. Pop, ladling out the last glasses of punch and sending a final tumblerful to Alphonse in the kitchen, cordially agreed.

'Feeling quite peckish,' he said and hoped everyone else was.

The evening had begun well, he thought, and most people were laughing as they left the bar and went into the *salle à manger*. Everyone seemed properly warmed up, companionable, and happy.

Even Iris Snow, who had eaten nothing but two cream crackers since twelve o'clock midday, felt like a canary.

After the cooling punch the softer, warmer touch of *melon au porto* was like a velvety caress. Everyone agreed that that had been very well-chosen. Full marks. Absolutely. Even the twins mopped it up in no time, asking what it was called.

'There it is on the menu,' Charley said. 'You can read it. *Melon au porto*. Melon with port wine.'

The menu cards had been specially printed in gold and Mademoiselle herself had also ordered little decorations of gold doves to be added at each corner. She had searched for a long time for some suitable symbol of marital love and had finally decided that doves were it.

'Porto! Porto! old mother Shorto! Diddlum dorto!' the twins started shouting, and a smiling Pop, for once, had no word of reprimand.

A light white wine of the Loire, a little dry, accompanied the sole. It was colder, if anything, than the punch had been. Charley said he thought they married very well together and Pop said Charley should know. Ma remarked that she thought the sole was the best bit of fish she'd had in France and Mademoiselle Dupont beamed. Pop was sorry about the chips, though, and was on the verge of saying so when he changed his mind and said:

'In front of snails anyway. Anybody want to change and have snails? Don't all speak at once. Twins? Snails?'

'You're a snail!' the twins said. 'You're a silly old snail! Snail, snail, put out your horn — '

Pop, with happy restraint, merely smiled and Mademoiselle Dupont, who had always known how correct, undemonstrative, and reserved the English were, couldn't help thinking that their children, at table, sometimes enjoyed the strangest latitude.

Under these pleasantries and the cold white wine of the Loire, Iris Snow began to feel more and more like a singing bird. Now and then she became conscious of one of her protuberances slipping a little under her brown dress and she gave it a bit of a hitch.

Angela Snow began to wonder if she'd got a

flea or something and gave her occasional looks of disapproval. She'd caught a flea once before at one of those wretched *pardons*. You never knew.

'And what's next? What's coming next?' Pop said, rubbing his hands. Things were going with a bang. 'The *rosbif*. Yes? No? I sink so — yes!'

The roast beef was presently wheeled in on a sort of large, ancient perambulator. It reposed there under a kind of silver shed. This had not been used for thirty years or so and, like the coffee filters, had gone rather brassy at the edges.

The wheeler-in was Alphonse, complete with white hat, white choker, a gravy spoon of about quart measure, and a carving knife two inches wide. His too large, too handsome eyes darted rapidly about the room like jets, catching Iris Snow in the act of doing a twitch. This he interpreted as a sign of secret recognition and took good note of it as he turned up the spirit flame that sprang out of the bowels of the perambulator to keep the beef warm.

Presently Alphonse was carving the *rosbif* with pride among rising steam and sizzling gravy. Every red slice came off with a lofty, dandyish flourish. The *pouding à la Jorkshire* was helped to the plates with a touch of fire and almost reverent extravagance — typical froggy, Pop thought.

Ma was given the first helping, Alphonse standing over her in a suspended bow to ask, in French, if madame would taste and pronounce judgement on the *pouding* please?

Mademoiselle Dupont translated this request with bilingual flutterings and Ma took a good mouthful of Yorkshire. Everyone waited in silence while she slipped it down. It wasn't half as good as she knocked up herself of a Sunday morning, she decided, but wasn't bad really and she said, in a strong English accent:

'Très bon. Very nice indeed. Très bon. Nice.' Ma speared a second piece of Yorkshire on the end of her fork and held it across the table to Pop. 'Better pass your judgement too, Pop, hadn't you?'

Pop, who was feeling in the mood to praise anything, even saucisson à la mode d'ici, accepted the pudding nippily and tasted it with a loud elastic smack of his lips. A moment later, searching for a word to describe what Alphonse had created, he was fired by a moment of happy inspiration, remembering a word the Brigadier had used.

'Delectable!' he said. 'Absolutely delectable. Hot stuff. Formidable!'

As if at a signal, Alphonse started to leap up and down, spontaneously brandishing the carving knife, at the same time darting flaming glances at Iris Snow, who twitched her bosom again in reply.

A moment later she was astounded to see Alphonse start careering round the table, waving the knife with sweeps of expert extravagance, as if he contemplated chasing her. A sudden transcendent thrill went through her, moving her strangely. It was all a dream. In imagination she suddenly saw herself being pursued by Alphonse over miles of Breton heather, among wild rocks, towards the sea, finally hiding herself from the

144

dark penetrative pursuing eyes in some far-distant *allée couverte*, among secret tumuli.

Mademoiselle Dupont was horrified. After a single second of relief that with the approval of the *pouding à la Jorkshire* the second of the night's ordeals was over, the first having been with the corset, she was now faced with the fact that Alphonse was about to have one of his temperamental fits. Something, as Pop remarked so often of Charley, must have got into him, and she could only think it was the large glass of *le punch* and two equally large *cognacs* that Pop had had sent into the kitchen for the purpose of encouraging him. It was too *terrible*, too *effrayant*, for words.

Ma, on the other hand, starting laughing like a drain. The children started shrieking too, especially Victoria, who was easily liable to accidents if she pitched her voice too high. Iris Snow was laughing loudly herself, uncertain what to do about the second transcendent thrill that went through her at an even faster, more ecstatically piercing pace than the first, making her quiver from throat to toe. All she could do was to giggle wildly whenever Alphonse brandished the knife, each time having a strange spasmodic recurrence of her dream.

Suddenly, after Alphonse had run round the table three or four times, the flame under the meat perambulator leapt up and then went out with an unseemly plop that sounded not at all unlike a belch. As if at a second signal Alphonse stopped running. Breathing hard, he abandoned the carving knife in order to relight the flame and in another second, as the glow sprang from beneath the brassy meat cover, Iris Snow experienced a third transcending rush of emotion that took her far beyond rocks and tumuli and even the roast beef and Yorkshire that everyone was now enjoying happily.

'I sank you, ladish and jentlemens,' Alphonse said. He had learned these few words of English off by heart from the second cook, who had once worked in Whitechapel. 'Blast and damn, *merci mesdames et messieurs*, blast and damn, sank you! *Vive les Anglais! Vive le Jorkshire!*'

At this he suddenly took off his tall chef's hat, raised it, bowed politely, and backed out of the *salle à manger*, giving a final dark undressing glance at Iris Snow, who was trying hard to conceal her emotion by hastily sliding Yorkshire pudding into her mouth. She was not very successful, though she had to admit to herself that she had tasted nothing like the rich red beef and its delicious melting pudding for years.

Rich food, even more than the unaccustomed punch, the port, the white wine, and the Chambolle Musigny that accompanied the beef, was now having a strange and unprecedented effect on her. Its stimulus was most marked where she might least have expected it. She was beginning to feel queer thumpings in the bosom, with sudden longings for air.

Her head on the other hand seemed quite light and clear. Her mind retained all its sane, rippling canary-like quality. She was sure she had been perfectly lucid as Alphonse constantly regarded her with those immense, buttery eyes. Alphonse, on the other hand, thought otherwise and had noted over and over again how often she twitched at him. It was very interesting, that twitch.

'I knew the French'd never do the custard and jelly properly,' Ma said in a whisper to Angela Snow, who was sitting between her and Pop. 'The custard's like billstickers' paste.'

Angela Snow said she thought the French didn't really know custard: as custard, that was.

'Then it's about time they did,' Ma said, with something like severity.

She was in fact merely tasting the jelly and custard for the children's sake while actually waiting for *crêpes Suzette* to come on.

It was past eleven o'clock when Alphonse arrived back from the kitchen to make the business of the *crêpes Suzette* a sacrifice of joy. That was the best part of the evening, Ma thought. So did the children, who sprang out of their chairs every time a pan of golden flame went up and shrieked that it was just like fireworks.

'Ought to have the lights out,' Ma suggested. 'Look very pretty.'

When the lights were put out the flares of flaming liqueurs danced about the darkened *salle à manger*. The bright leaping light gave to the front of Angela Snow's skin-tight dress a remarkable effect of transformation. Her body looked no longer blue but silver and it would have been almost too much for Mademoiselle Dupont to bear if Pop, who was sitting next to her, hadn't thought it as good a moment as any to caress her thigh.

After that the dinner never seemed quite the

same to her again. She gradually lost all hope of concentration. From that moment she never knew whether it was the fourth bottle of Chambolle Musigny they were drinking, or the fifth or what it was. In contrast to Iris Snow she had begun to feel quite light-headed and there was still champagne to come.

It came at twelve o'clock, together with the cake that Alphonse had made. Alphonse, more buttery-eyed than ever, bore the cake into the *salle à manger* himself and set it down, with pride and a flourish, before Mariette and Charley.

The cake was iced in bright soapy pink, with a single large red candle on it, and on top of it were the words imprinted circularwise, in red:

HAPPY BIRDSDAY ANNIVERSAIRE
AND GOOD LOOK

When she read these words Ma felt very touched and then everyone toasted Mariette and Charley in champagne. Even M. Mollet had crept out of hiding again, mole-like and shy, to take part in the toasting, staring with filmy eyes at the blue vision of Angela Snow that had troubled him so much, and so increasingly, ever since he had first seen it at eight o'clock.

All through the toasting, Pop stood with swelling paternal pride, watching Mariette. No doubt about it, she was sumptuous: even more beautiful, he thought, than Ma had once been. Charley boy was lucky all right and Pop could only hope that he would, in the shortest possible time, show his appreciation of the fact in the right and proper way. Pop couldn't help thinking too of the day, perhaps, not all that far ahead, when Primrose, Victoria, and the twins would begin to develop too on those same impressive, luscious lines. Perhaps by that time Mariette and even Montgomery would be having children and — who knows? — him and Ma following suit again. He was all set for that. That would be the day.

As if in answer to his thoughts, as the hotel's old brassy gramophone started playing for dancing, he heard a soft voice say:

'Wouldn't you dance with me, Pop? I'd love to have the first dance with you.'

It was Primrose. There was an indefinable half-sad smile on her face, the sadness heightened by the fact that she had, Pop thought, put just the faintest touch of lipstick on and had crimped her dark hair down over her forehead in a curious little fringe, in the way the French girls did.

Course he would dance, he told her, and she at once held up her slim sun-brown arms, again with a touch of sadness, the fingers rather drooping.

'Thought you wouldn't ask me,' she said sadly as he swung her away to the tune of an old favourite, *La Vie en Rose*, 'I've been hoping you would.'

Pop said he was sorry and also that it hadn't struck him that he'd been expected to ask his own daughter to dance. Laughing merrily, he said he reckoned she ought to have asked him.

'Oh! no,' she said and again the voice was full

of her plaintive sadness, 'I couldn't do that. Pop, it just shows how much you know.'

Oh! and what about? Pop asked her.

'Women.'

It was some seconds before Pop recovered from this withering blow. When he finally did so he suddenly thought it diplomatic to side-step a second one — in case one should be coming — by neatly changing the subject with a ripple of a laugh.

'Well, home tomorrow. Old home sweet home.'

Primrose, unsmiling, wasn't deceived a bit and showed it by looking him full in the face, her dark soft eyes full of sad disapprobation.

'Why do you have to sound so glad about it?'

Glad? Pop said. Glad? Why not? It was nice to go on holiday but it was nicer still to go home. Everybody said so.

'Everybody?' she said. 'Who's everybody? What do they know?'

Pop, unable to think of a sensible answer to this crushing question, found himself looking down at his daughter's bright yellow dress. He was surprised to find it cut rather wide and low at the neck, where she was wearing a double row of pearls. He was even more surprised to discover that the body underneath it was no longer quite that of a little girl, and that she had beautiful little salt cellars, very like Angela Snow's, just at the base of her olive neck, where the pearls were.

'Don't you want to go home?' he said.

He was up against it now all right, he thought.

He remembered what Ma had said. He'd got a handful now.

'No, Pop,' she said. 'That's it. I didn't sleep a wink all last night for thinking about it. Nor the night before. Nor the night before that.'

Pop, in his airy way, said for crying out gently whatever was it that had done that to her? For the life of him he couldn't imagine.

'Pop,' she said and again she looked up at him, this time no longer with sadness but with a glance so swift that it had swung away again before he could catch it, leaving him looking down at nothing but the dark oval of her hair. She had very pretty hair and it curled fluffily in the nape of her neck, just like Ma's did. 'I want to ask you something.'

Ask on, Pop said. Fire away. Money, he supposed.

'Pop,' she said and her voice was sad again, with something like low passion in it, 'do I *have* to go home? *Must* I go home?'

Didn't mean to tell him she wanted to stay here, in France, did she? Pop said. All on her lonesome? All by herself?

'Not by myself,' she said. 'I won't be alone.'

It wouldn't be much fun in the hotel, he reminded her. The season was practically over.

'I'll have someone to stay with,' she said.

Before answering Pop permitted himself the luxury of humming a few bars of *La Vie en Rose*. Very good song, *La Vie en Rose*. Good thing Mademoiselle Dupont had fished out some of these old favourites. They got you.

'Oh?' he said. 'Who?'

'My boy-friend.'

For once unsurprised, Pop was back as quick as a bird, laughing.

'Thought you had two?' he said.

Pained dark eyes held him for a sharp second or two, but whether in renewed sadness or sheer scorn for his brief burst of laughter and the little he understood about women he simply never knew.

'I've given one up,' she said. 'I had to. I had to make the decision.'

Though he'd always held that there was safety in numbers, Pop hummed what he thought were a few consolatory, approving murmurs, mostly mere wordless echoes from *La Vie en Rose*, but somehow they didn't seem to impress her. She was silent for once, unconsoled.

'What's this one's name?' he said.

'Marc-Antoine.'

Typical Froggy, Pop thought. Very fancy.

'And how old's he?'

'A year older than me. Twelve.'

'H'm,' Pop said, heavily, quite unlike himself. 'H'm.'

A second later he found himself looking down at her, but she at once looked away.

'He says I can go and live with him,' she said.

'Eh?' Pop said. He spoke faintly. Good grief, bit early wasn't it? He knew from experience that Ma had been well forward and all that for her age, but dammit. After all, there were limits —

'I mean with his parents. His father keeps a confectioner's shop. A *pâtisserie*. I could — Oh please, Pop' — suddenly he couldn't help

152

thinking that the voice was uncannily, disturbingly like that of the loveliest and most insinuating of all his daughters, Mariette — 'please, Pop, couldn't I? Please?'

Pop, giving what he thought was a sagacious wag of the head, a gesture meant to be taken seriously, said simply:

'You'd better ask your Ma.'

Primrose, who like Mariette wasn't her father's daughter for nothing, was back as quick as a swallow.

'I asked her. She said I was to ask you.'

Cornered, Pop took refuge in a few further light bars of *La Vie en Rose*, but he knew that that lark couldn't go on much longer. There was a crisis about somewhere.

'Well, I don't know,' he said, his voice heavy again. What the devil could he say? He simply didn't know. He could only wonder, in an unprofound moment, what Ma would say? Perhaps Ma didn't know either? 'Well, I don't know — '

Profounder instincts than his own kept Primrose silent. She hadn't even another pleading, imploring please to offer and he knew he was in a spot.

'This wants thinking about,' he told her in another heavy but not very deep excursion — dammit, what was all that psychology lark that Ma talked about? Didn't that come in somewhere? With something like a flurry of desperation, utterly unusual in him, he made an effort to sum up the kernel of the matter in a single phrase and came out with half a dozen words of brave simplicity that struck even him as being not quite what was wanted: 'Long way from home, you know.'

A second later she withered him with a glance both needle-like and wretched. Really downright wretched. He expected any moment to see big, sorrowful tears welling from her eyes. That would be the end. That would get him. Dammit, he was slap in the middle of it now all right.

'It's all very well for you,' she said. Somebody had turned the record over or put on another one and now the gramophone was playing a tune he didn't know at all, but which Primrose did — a heart-twister of yearning southern sorrow called *Anima Core*. 'You're grown up. You've forgotten about things — '

Pop started to assure her that there were some things he hadn't forgotten about yet, but she said peremptorily:

'You'd like to part us, I expect.'

'Well, I — '

'Don't you ever hear that bit Charley's always quoting?' she said. 'It's his favourite bit. '*Love is not love that alters when it alteration finds,*' — we have it at school too sometimes.'

Pop was silent. That feller Keats again. Charley-boy all over. He had to hand it to Charley. Terrific influence on the family that chap had been. No doubt about it.

Gloom hung over him like a cloud and he was profoundly wishing he knew a bit more about psychology, if not Keats, when a cheerful languid voice hailed him and said:

'Why the dark deep furrowed brow, dear boy?

154

The *crêpes Suzette* not settling or what? or shouldn't a girl ask? Cheer up, chum.'

It was Angela Snow, dancing past him with Montgomery, and Pop, suddenly restored to his perky, normal self again, laughed back in typical rousing fashion.

'Only Juliet here,' he said, stroking Primrose's soft dark hair — dammit, he wasn't sure he wasn't very nearly quoting Keats or Shakespeare or somebody himself now, ' — wants to stay in France with her Romeo.'

'And rightly so,' Angela Snow said. 'Got the right idea. You're going to let her, of course, aren't you? I'll kick you if you don't.'

'Course,' Pop said. 'Course. Got to start sometime.'

'Sensible man,' she said. 'Anyway I'll be here for a while yet. I'll do a chaperone.'

Unstartled by a word only vaguely familiar to him, Pop watched the turquoise, willowy vision float away and then found himself, a moment later, looking down at a pair of dark eyes brimming over, as he had feared they would be, with tears — except that they were now clear, bright tears of joy.

'Oh! Pop,' was all Primrose could say. 'Oh! Pop. Marc-Antoine will be thrilled.'

French blood in the family now, Pop thought. Blimey, what next?

'It's just like *The Sugar Plum Fairy*,' Primrose said softly, her olive lids quite closed. 'I never imagined — '

'Like *who*?' Pop said.

'Tchaikowsky.'

155

She was light-headed, Pop thought. Must be. It did that to you when you were young. You went off your grub and got to thinking you were floating about, empty.

He now hadn't the vaguest idea what his daughter, with eyes still lusciously closed, was talking about and he decided it could only be another of them larks they learnt you nowadays at school. And again, as if sensing his thoughts, she said:

'It's about the little girl who goes to bed after a Christmas party and can't sleep and then comes downstairs and watches *The Sugar Plum Fairy* dance and all that. Just like this. Haven't you ever heard of it?'

Pop had to confess he hadn't. Bit out of his range, like that feller Keats and the rest of 'em. Nevertheless he was fascinated, as always, by the hint of an excursion into new upper worlds and asked her what else they learnt them nowadays at school? You never knew.

'Oh! biology,' she said. 'Sex and all that.'

For crying out gently, he thought. No wonder Ma had said she was developing early. It didn't surprise him, considering the help they got. Again, for the second or third time, he didn't know what to say and was saved the necessity of attempting any comment by another airy remark from Primrose, delivered this time with dark eyes fully open, roundly staring up at him, beautifully glistening.

'They don't teach them sex in French schools though,' she said.

'Oh?' Pop said, 'don't they? Well, well. Too

bad.' He laughed in his customary rousing fashion. He'd had an idea for a long time the Froggies were a backward lot. Even in sex. How did she know they didn't teach it?

'Because I asked Marc-Antoine,' she said. 'He was awfully surprised we had it.'

Didn't wonder at it, Pop thought. Didn't wonder at all.

'Anyway he was very interested and that's how we started to get to know each other better.'

He must tell Ma all this. Ma would certainly have to hear all about this lark, Pop was thinking. At the same time he was wondering if another glass of champagne wouldn't do him all the good in the world, when suddenly the music stopped.

In the short ensuing silence he saw Ma talking to one of the French chambermaids. He guessed little Oscar was awake and was quite certain of it a moment later when he heard Ma say she'd be up in a minute to soothe him down and that if punch, white wine, red wine, champagne, and *crêpe Suzette* wouldn't do the trick nothing would.

With an involuntary rush of paternal affection he turned to pat Primrose on the head and was astonished to find that he stood with empty arms. A voice low with emotion thanked him with a few happy whispered syllables for the dance and everything. He stood without a coherent thought he could offer in answer, trying hazily to disentangle all that stuff about Sugar Plum Fairies, Tchaikowsky, sex, biology, and what they learnt you nowadays in school, so bemused that he probably wouldn't have heard

157

the next record, which was that old favourite *Night and Day* if it hadn't been that a curious thing occurred.

As Iris Snow heard the opening bars of the music something suspiciously like a sob sprang from her throat. A moment later she hastily pressed a tiny lace square of handkerchief to her mouth and started rushing from the room.

★   ★   ★

By one o'clock Pop had danced once each with Mariette, Ma, and Angela Snow and was now having a waltz with Mademoiselle Dupont. Ma warned him several times of the virtues of equal shares.

'Got to treat all of us the same,' she said. 'It's Iris Snow after Mademoiselle Dupont. No favouritism. Don't forget.'

Pop, who was ready to distribute favours everywhere, remarked that Iris Snow had disappeared somewhere and laughingly supposed she might have gone off to catch the flea.

'What flea?' Ma said.

Pop explained how Angela Snow, who was increasingly irritated by her sister, had jocularly told him about the twitch.

'Not a very nice thing to say,' Ma said. 'Still, don't you catch it though.'

He left her to find Mademoiselle Dupont, who was in excited mood. While she danced she kept breathing harder and harder and as the dance went on she threw back her head, laughing freely, and said she felt like singing.

Rather to Pop's surprise she actually burst into a few bars of song. Her voice came out as a rather pleasant not uncultured contralto and not a bit as if she had adenoids, as French singers often do. Pop then said jovially that he felt like having a bit of a warble himself and on the spur of the moment suggested she should join him in *It Had To Be You* — but she didn't know that masterpiece, a favourite of Pop's youth, and they sang *C'est si bon* instead, she singing the French and he, in a light falsetto, what he could remember of the English words. Soon everyone else was singing too and the bright noise was punctuated by the cracking volley of champagne corks.

Iris Snow could hear them as she stood on the terrace outside, talking to Alphonse, in French, under the plane trees. Every moment she felt more than ever like a wild canary. She had never had so much to drink in her life and in rapid sentences she was telling Alphonse how much she adored his country. France was her mecca. Everything about France was so cultured. There was nowhere in the world like France. She adored it, its people, its art, its manners, its wine, and its food.

From a woman who fed largely on soft-boiled eggs, dry toast, and anchovy paste on biscuits this was said with a remarkable degree of passion, and in the lights of the hotel windows Alphonse kept her held with remorseless charm in the overlarge handsome eyes that were now so like big, shining prunes.

Soon she was aware again of a transcendent

rushing thrill, that strange, unsteady thumping in the bosom and the panting desire for air. She longed to rush down to the beach, she said. A few moments later Alphonse guided her unsteadily to the *plage*, where she found it much easier to sit down than stand up and where she suddenly found herself remarking recklessly, for no reason at all, in a voice that seemed not to belong to her, that the night was just like Grecian honey. It was all like new warm honey from the south, she said, and she longed to rush to the sea. A moment later she started to take off her shoes and stockings, going about it so ineptly that Alphonse, without asking, started to give help with the suspenders.

With a protesting shriek of joy she suddenly dashed across the beach to the sea. The little pleated phosphorescent waves were just like milk, she thought, and over in the western sky a great star — Oh! no, a planet, she supposed — was hanging like burnt gold above the sea — oh! so like a wonderful great big gingerbread, she called out crazily, with all the gilt still on!

Alphonse, who hadn't the vaguest idea what she was talking about, pursued her to the edge of the water. By the time he reached it she was already paddling, ecstatically westwards, up to her knees. With the water rising up her legs she suddenly decided to tuck her frock in her knickers, which were the same shade of dull coffee brown as the dress. Seeing this, Alphonse started to take off his shoes and stockings too and roll up the legs of his blue and white striped chef's trousers, which Iris adored.

At this point the sea, as Charley had once explained, was shallow for half a mile from the shore, and Iris was still only up to her knees, thirty yards out, when Alphonse caught up with her. He at once embraced her passionately round the lower middle and started kissing her madly on one ear.

In the middle of this she felt her knees buckle underneath her. In a moment she was up to her armpits, kneeling on sand. Alphonse went under too and in this uncomfortable position, still crying out that the night was like honey and the stars like gilded gingerbread, Iris Snow surrendered gladly to whatever was coming, with low sobs of joy.

* * *

Back in the hotel, while Alphonse was also making the interesting discovery that the English could be surprisingly unrestrained, Mademoiselle Dupont was taking advantage of Ma's absence upstairs to invite Pop into the Bureau. There was something of importance she wished to say.

With shining eyes she asked him to accept a small green leather box from her.

'A small thing. A little parting gift for you.'

Opening the box, Pop found inside it a pair of silver cuff-links reposing on a bed of emerald velvet.

'Please to look. There is something — '

Pop took the cuff-links out and, looking more closely, found that Mademoiselle Dupont had

had his initials engraved on the faces of the links in the form of a monogram.

'Very nice,' he said. 'Absolutely perfick — '

'It is just a small thing. Just — '

'Wonderful. Very *chic*,' he went on and said he didn't know how to thank her. '*Très snob*.'

Mademoiselle Dupont, without saying so, very much hoped he would thank her by kissing her and in fact he did. The kiss was of a kind she had never experienced before and presently knew that she probably never would do again. Under the long extremely well-directed pressure she several times thought the new corset would give way.

When it was all over she stood looking up at him with unsteady luminous eyes, holding his face in her hands.

'Tomorrow you will be back in England,' she said. 'Tell me about your house in England. Your *château*.'

Oh! it was perfick, Pop said. A paradise. You wouldn't find anything more perfick in the world nowhere, he told her, and then in that glowing hyper-sensory way of his warmed up to the business of describing how the junk-yard was in spring, with cuckoos calling, nightingales going glorious hell for leather night and day in the bluebell wood, water lilies gold and white in the stream, fields glowing with strawberries, meadows rich with buttercups and grasses, and all the rest of the marvellous, mad, midsummer lark in England.

For some time she listened to all this as she might have listened to some sort of celestial revelation and then decided to ask a question. It was perhaps a rather indelicate question, but she knew that if she didn't ask it now she never would.

'And will you perhaps marry one day?'

Pop patted her playfully on the roundest part of the corset with an especially warm affectionate hand, and laughed loudly. Mademoiselle Dupont had never known hands so warm.

'Shall if somebody asks me.'

'Someone will,' she told him with transfixed, shining eyes. 'I'm sure that someone will.'

Better give her the other half, Pop thought, and set the seal on the evening, the gift and her complete and luminous joy by repeating the kiss at even greater length, under even greater pressure.

'I have decided to reconstruct the hotel,' she said. 'To have an *ascenseur* and water hot and cold in all the bedrooms. It was you who gave me such ideas.'

That was the spirit, Pop said. *Très snob.* Pull 'em down. Start afresh. He wouldn't mind putting a bit of money into it himself if it could be wangled.

'We could be partners?' she said.

'Could be,' Pop said. 'Could be.'

'It is always you,' she said, 'who has such wonderful ideas. Before you came to stay here I had no courage for such changes — '

'Courage my foot,' Pop said and gave the corset a final semi-stroking amorous pat in the roundest part. 'Natural. If you want an apple off the tree go and get the damn thing.'

163

Still pondering on this remark as if it were some mysterious, mystical text for living, Mademoiselle Dupont went back with Pop to the *salle à manger*, where everyone except Angela Snow and M. Mollet was still dancing.

In an astonished spasm of jealousy Angela Snow watched her come into the room, holding Pop in a kind of aerial embrace of wonder. For a few electrified seconds she experienced an amazing impulse to rush over and smack Mademoiselle Dupont's face as hard as she could.

While she was still trying to resist it something surprising occurred. She suddenly found herself being asked to dance by M. Mollet.

M. Mollet had wanted to ask her to dance all evening but had lacked the courage. Now, shy and flushed, pince-nez sparkling, he began dancing with her in a way she hadn't experienced before. He held her consistently at arm's length, as if afraid of letting the front of his body touch the long sheath-like curves of hers. He was several inches shorter than she was, which meant that he was constantly forced to gaze up at her. In this way she found herself concentrating on his eyes. Behind the glasses the pupils were a peculiar mid-shade of brown, like partly roasted coffee beans. They were sad, mute, appealingly funny little eyes and suddenly she liked them.

After a speechless five minutes she suddenly felt a dreamy and extra-ordinary impulse to kiss M. Mollet bang in the centre of the forehead. Fortunately the music stopped a moment later, waking her.

'And a damn good thing too,' she thought. 'If

164

you'd have kissed him the poor dear would have dropped down dead. Don't be so lethal.'

In a second all her flippancy was back. The jealous creature who had wanted to slap Mademoiselle Dupont's face had disappeared.

Meanwhile, on the far side of the room, in the electric light, the delicate little prisms of Ma's diamanté comb flashed with many colours as Pop paused to joke with her.

'It's time you had another dance with Angela,' she told him. 'Fair's fair.'

It was nearly four o'clock, Pop reminded her. He wanted to sit down with a quiet glass of champagne somewhere. Even he was getting tired.

'Do as I say,' Ma said. 'Have one more dance with her and then get into bed.'

Pop threw back his head and laughed uproariously.

'Ma,' he said, 'I think you'd better say that sentence in some other way, hadn't you?'

Ma shrieked, digging him joyfully in the ribs, realizing what she had said.

A moment later Pop found himself dancing with the same languid, casual, flippant vision who had long since endeared herself to him as a sporting, kindred spirit.

She, as if unable to recover from M. Mollet's technique of dancing at arm's length, let Pop hold her in that way too, looking straight into his happy, perky eyes and giving him a sporting wink or two.

'Well?'

'Well?' Pop said.

'Whale of a party.'

Pop said he thought so too and she said:

'One thing missing, though.'

'Oh?'

'That proposal.'

'From me?'

'From you,' she said. 'Very nearly too late now. I've practically given myself to M. Mollet.'

'Have a heart,' Pop said. 'For crying out gently.'

'Love him. Adore him,' she said. 'He's sweet. Surprised?'

Pop admitted he was very surprised but remarked that there was no accounting for tastes.

'But I do, dear boy,' she said. 'He's so small. And moley. And brown and all that. One wants to hug the wretched man. Don't you fathom?'

Pop said he didn't fathom and told her, much to her surprise, that he thought it was a clear case of psychology. It was something she'd missed somewhere at some time or never had. See?

For answer she drew him nearer and laid her lovely head on his shoulder.

'This I wouldn't have missed for all the world,' she said, 'for all the world, my sweet. For all the world I wouldn't have missed it. It's been absolutely perfick. But then with you it always would be.'

Impulsively she kissed him as she had wanted to kiss M. Mollet, in the centre of the forehead, and an astonished Pop almost recoiled from a display of a technique with which he had been totally unacquainted before.

'That's for keeps,' she said, in a whisper. 'Don't lose it, will you?'

Half an hour later the party was over. Nobody in the hotel was awake except M. Mollet, who had been so shattered by the evening's experiences that he was busy taking aspirin, and Mademoiselle Dupont, who lay full length on her bed in darkness, still in her corset, thinking over and over again of how she would reshape the hotel, put in an *ascenseur* and hot and cold water in all the bedrooms and how, perhaps, she might have a partner; and also of the fogless splendours of an England astonishingly revealed as abounding in strawberries, cuckoos, water-lilies, nightingales, and *pouding à la Jorkshire*.

Outside the hotel nobody was awake either; except Iris Snow, who was walking slowly up and down the *plage*, watching the setting planet that was so like a gingerbread with all the gilt still on, trying to find a pair of lost stockings and all the time singing a happy bare-foot song.

9

In the morning Angela Snow woke at eleven o'clock with a headache. She had been a miserable meanie about Mademoiselle Dupont, she thought, and it wasn't like her. She felt very, very cross with herself. And without breakfasting or waking Iris, who hadn't come in till six o'clock, she went down into the town and ordered two dozen roses to be sent to Mademoiselle Dupont in the afternoon. There was nothing she could think of to say as a message and she sent them without a card.

Then she decided to go and say goodbye to the Larkins and then, a moment later, impulsively decided not to after all. Enough, after all, was as good as a feast. It was all over now and she could only send them a silent, sporting blessing, thinking as she did of the long, golden, light-headed afternoon on the dunes, when salt and sun had burned her lips and the blown breath of sea and pines had been strong enough to make her even happier and tipsier than Pop's cocktails and the wine had done.

The result was that when the Rolls finally drew away from the Beau Rivage at half past one only two people besides Mademoiselle Dupont and M. Mollet, furtive as ever, stood on the terrace, under the plane trees, to wave goodbye. Like two silent torch bearers, Primrose and Marc-Antoine stood solemnly holding large pink-and-chocolate ice-creams in bright saffron-coloured cornets, giving the tops of them occasional licks with bright pink tongues. Neither of them uttered a single syllable in farewell and after Pop had been struck once again by the dubious distant prospect of having French blood in the family he couldn't help noticing that Marc-Antoine, who was the colour of suet and wore large shining steel-rimmed spectacles, looked remarkably like a younger, smaller, froggier Mr Charlton. Funny how his daughters attracted the type.

When everything was finally packed and everyone was in the car — Ma quite imperial in the back, with little Oscar in her arms — Pop went up to the steps of the hotel and under the astonished eyes of M. Mollet gave Mademoiselle Dupont a prolonged parting sample of amorous affection that even had the children cheering from the car.

'Here, stand back and let the dog see the rabbit!' Ma called.

'*Au revoir!*' Pop said. 'Goodbye, Mademoiselle,' and at last retreated from her dazed figure with several debonair waves of the hand. '*À bientôt! Au revoir, merci!* So long! Goodbye.'

'Goodbye!' she called. '*Au revoir!* Goodbye! *Adieu!*'

'Goodbye! *Au revoir!*' everyone called. '*Adieu. Goodbye!*'

When Pop got back into the Rolls even Ma had to confess she was surprised at the length and generosity of Pop's prolonged farewell.

'You wouldn't be if you'd seen the bill,' Pop said. 'Dammit, might as well have my money's worth.'

The bill was a blinder. He doubted very much if he'd ever get over the bill. Percentages for this, taxes for that, services for the other. Breathing charges. He doubted if even Charley, that master of figures, would ever be able to sort out all the dodgy squeezes in that bill. It had very nearly skinned him out, he told Ma, very nearly skinned him.

'Think we got enough to get home with?' Ma said.

'Might have to pawn the Rolls,' Pop said serenely. 'Well, so much for the French lark.'

Still, he thought a moment later, it was all over, it was well wurf it, and he gave a final chorus of contrapuntal toots of the horn in debonair farewell as the Rolls moved away.

As soon as the Rolls was out of sight and Pop's cheerful tooting of first the melodious tune of the country horn and then the symphonic brass of the town one had died away Mademoiselle Dupont rushed back into the hotel, determined that no one should detect the tears in her eyes. But when the red roses arrived at two o'clock there was no help for it and she lay for the rest of the afternoon on her bed, weepily watching the roses in their big glass vase and seeing over and over again the pictures Pop had painted for her of his home, his *château*, the lordly paradise, in England. Never again would she say that the English were frigid and reticent or restrained or that they took their pleasures sadly or that fog perpetually covered their land. She knew it to be otherwise.

Meanwhile, as the Rolls drove along the coast,

Ma called Pop through the speaking-tube.

'I don't know what you did to Mademoiselle Dupont last night but you got her in a proper tizzy.'

'Nothing,' Pop said airily. 'Nothing. Not a thing.'

'Did you ask her to marry you?'

Pop said he rather thought he had. Hadn't he ought to have done? Ma wasn't offended? After all she'd given him the cuff-links. Had to encourage her a bit.

'Oh! it's not that,' Ma said and started laughing in her customary hearty fashion. 'I was only thinking I hope she don't have to wait as long as I have.'

Pop burst out laughing too. That was one of Ma's good ones. Well, bill or no bill, it had been a pretty good holiday. Done everybody a whale of good, he thought, getting to know how foreigners lived. Especially Mariette and Charley, who both looked in the pink. He'd expect results now.

'I expect you asked Angela too, didn't you?' Ma said down the tube.

'Shouldn't wonder,' Pop said. 'She said summat about it.'

Ma said she wasn't worried about Angela. She was a sport. She could take care of herself. But she didn't want Pop going round putting people in a tizzy and breaking their hearts. You'd got to draw the line somewhere.

Pop agreed, but still when you were in Rome —

'Oh! talking about Rome, there's another

171

thing,' Ma said. 'Have you thought any more about little Oscar's names?'

Pop was quick to confess he hadn't.

'Well, I know you've been busy, but we can't let the poor little mite go about all his life with only one name, can we?' Ma said. 'That would be a nice thing, wouldn't it?'

Terrible, Pop said.

'Well, I've been thinking a lot about it. Are you listening?'

Yes, Pop told her on the tube, he was listening.

'Well,' Ma said, 'I tell you what.'

'Half a minute. We want something good. Something special. No half larks. Something a bit *très snob*.'

'I know that,' Ma said. 'Anyway I've thought what I'd like to call him.'

'Oh?' Pop said. 'What?'

'I thought we'd call him Oscar Livingstone David Larkin.'

Pop was silent for some moments. All his strong paternal instincts came steeping warmly to the surface as he contemplated the proposed trio of names for his son. The names had got to be right, he thought again, no half larks.

Almost immediately he had a qualm about it and called back to Ma down the tube:

'No, Ma. Won't do. Not them. Can't have them.'

'Oh?' Ma said. 'Why not?'

'Makes his initials O.L.D.,' Pop said. 'He'll be called Old Larkin all his life. Can't have that.'

Ma cordially agreed; they couldn't possibly have that; and before she could think of anything else to say Pop called her again on the tube.

'Giving us a bit of trouble, this one,' he said. 'Good job it wasn't twins,' and went on to shoot a sudden, uneasily pertinent question at Charley. 'Twins run in your family, Charley old man?'

Not that he knew of, Charley said.

'Well they do in ours!' Pop said in direct, open challenge, 'you want to watch what you're up to.'

And what did that mean? Ma said. Watch what who was up to?

'Well, you know,' Pop said darkly. 'Somebody or other.'

Mr Charlton treated these exchanges with silence, not only because it was a silence he thought they deserved but also because he couldn't for the life of him think of anything remotely sensible to say.

'What was that you said about Rome, Ma?' Pop said. 'Didn't you say once you wanted to call him after some Roman Emperor?'

'I did an' all,' Ma said. 'But I'm blowed if I can remember which one it was now. Tiberius, I think.'

Back in a flash of scolding breath came Charley:

'Not on your life. Not that one. Not on your nelly.'

'Why not?' Ma said.

'You'd hardly want to call him after a judicial murderer, do you?'

Charley at it again, Pop thought, in silent admiration. Charley away again. Amazing feller. You never knew where Charley was off to next. He certainly used his loaf sometimes.

'I should think not,' Ma said. 'He's got a soft nature, this boy. Wasn't there one called Octavius, though? I remember him on telly once. In a play.'

'You can't possibly call him Octavius,' Charley said. 'He's the seventh, not the eighth.'

'Who is?' Pop said.

'Oscar. Besides Oscar Octavius sounds a bit much, don't you think? Call him Septimus if you want a Roman name.'

'Septimus?' Ma said. 'Why Septimus?'

'Septimus — the seventh. Sept — the same as in French. The same as September. The seventh month.'

Mariette, who occasionally found it necessary to keep Charley in check, he was so clever sometimes, said quickly:

'September isn't the seventh month, lovey. It's the ninth.'

Back in a revelatory flash came Charley again:

'Ah! but it used to be, darling, before the calendar was changed. Just as November used to be the ninth and December the tenth.'

Pop was stunned again to silent admiration. Wonderfully clever feller, Charley. Terrific clever feller. No keeping up with Charley.

'I think Septimus sounds rather nice,' Ma said, kissing Oscar on the ear, 'it suits his nature. You like it, Pop?'

He did, Pop said. It had that rather *très snob* touch about it. What Charley sometimes called the *je ne sais quoi*.

'Not too difficult?' Ma said. 'After all we want to give him names people can say.'

Pop treated this remark with a short soft laugh of scorn. What was the name of that kid at the post office? he wanted to know. Horsa or something, wasn't it? Septimus was no worse than that. Who was Horsa anyway?

'Saxon King,' Charley said blandly. 'Had a brother named Hengist.'

Altogether too taken aback to speak, Pop could only silently congratulate Ma on the swiftness with which she once again made one of her nippy changes of subject.

'What was the name of that other explorer?' Ma said and then started laughing inconsequently, thinking of Charley. It would certainly be a bomb under Charley if Mariette had twins. That would make him use his loaf a bit. They could call them Hengist and Horsa too.

'Who?' Pop said. 'Shackleton?'

'No, before him,' Ma said. 'A foreigner.'

The word foreigner struck a certain discord in Pop, who found himself silent again, thinking hard but at a loss. Again Ma couldn't think of the name she wanted either and it was Charley who at last, as so often before, came to the rescue.

'Columbus. Is that the one you've got in mind?'

Columbus, Ma said. Of course. That was it.

'Oscar Columbus,' Pop repeated several times over. 'That's got class. Oscar Columbus. That's a bit of *très snob*, an' all, Ma. I like that.'

Ma said she liked it too and should they settle on Oscar Septimus Columbus David then?

'Oh! not David,' Mariette said. 'I hate David.'

Pop confessed he too wasn't all that gone on David either and urged Ma to put her thinking cap on. Ma was always the one who had the brain waves. She was a dabster for names.

Less than half a minute later Ma confirmed Pop's faith in her by laughing merrily down the tube and saying she wasn't sure but she thought she'd got it.

'How about Dupont?' she said. 'Oscar Columbus Septimus Dupont Larkin?'

It tickled him to death, Pop said. Dupont — just the job. Perfick. It absolutely tickled him to death. *Très snob*.

'That's that then,' Ma said calmly. 'And if we can't have a wedding when we get home, at least we can have a christening, can't we? Fair enough?'

Fair enough, Pop said. Any excuse for a party.

'And I tell you something else I just thought of,' Ma said.

Oh? Pop wanted to know. What was that?

'I thought we'd ask Mademoiselle Dupont to be godmother,' she said. 'Sort of bring her into the family.'

That was a corker, Pop said. He wondered what Mademoiselle would think of that?

'Blessed if I know,' Ma said. 'You never can tell what these Frenchwomen are thinking, I always say,' and then realized why. 'After all I don't suppose you can if you don't know their language, can you?'

A moment later the thought of little Oscar having a French godmother set Pop slapping his knee and roaring with laughter. Joyful noises gurgled down the speaking-tube and the sound of the Rolls's contrapuntal horns rang royally across the rocky slopes of heather, somewhere among which Charley's beloved little train, symbol of travel long ago, seemed to let out a terse and mocking toot in reply.

'Godmother Dupont,' Pop said. 'Well, I'll go to the bone-house. I'll go to the ossuary.'

'Which,' Ma told him blandly but not uncordially, down the tube, 'is just about where you'll end up one of these fine days,' and then, with a sigh, settled serenely back on the Rolls's deep dove-grey cushions, a wide handsome spread of maternal bosom exposed, ready to give Oscar Columbus Septimus Dupont Larkin a little drop of the best.

We do hope that you have enjoyed reading this large print book.

Did you know that all of our titles are available for purchase?

We publish a wide range of high quality large print books including:
Romances, Mysteries, Classics
General Fiction
Non Fiction and Westerns

Special interest titles available in large print are:
The Little Oxford Dictionary
Music Book
Song Book
Hymn Book
Service Book

Also available from us courtesy of Oxford University Press:
Young Readers' Dictionary
(large print edition)
Young Readers' Thesaurus
(large print edition)

For further information or a free brochure, please contact us at:
Ulverscroft Large Print Books Ltd.,
The Green, Bradgate Road, Anstey,
Leicester, LE7 7FU, England.
Tel: (00 44) 0116 236 4325
Fax: (00 44) 0116 234 0205

THE DARLING BUDS OF MAY

H. E. Bates

The Larkin family — Pop, Ma, and their brood of six children — reside with a thriving menagerie on a small farm, where they live and love in amiable chaos. Rattling around in a gentian-blue thirty-hundredweight truck, doing a little of this and a little of that — picking fruit in the summer and hops in the autumn, wheeler-dealing, selling flowers at the roadside — they revel in life's simple pleasures. Then along comes Mr Cedric Charlton from the Inland Revenue, determined to assess the tax owed by Pop. But his plans are thrown into confusion by the eldest Larkin daughter — the entrancing Mariette . . .

WHEN THE GREEN WOODS LAUGH

H. E. Bates

City stockbroker Mr Jerebohm and his wife are seeking a rural retreat where they can host shooting parties and afternoon tea on the lawn. So Pop Larkin — junk dealer, family man, and Dragon's Blood connoisseur — sells them Gore Court, a crumbling pile of a country mansion, for a tidy profit. Now he can build his family that swimming pool they want. But the Larkins' new neighbours aren't quite so accepting of country ways — especially Pop's little eccentricities. And it's not long before a wobbly boat, a misplaced pair of hands, and Mrs Jerebohm's behind have Pop up before a magistrate . . .